HOW I STARTED THE APOCALYPSE

Brian Pinkerton

With apologies to

Richard Matheson and George Romero

Introduction
By Hugh Howey

I was in middle school when I first became obsessed with death, with the idea that one day I wouldn't exist. At the time, I thought something was wrong with me, that I was overly morbid. I would lie in bed at night and become petrified that I might fall asleep and never wake up. Closing my eyes, I would picture a dark place where I would one day live forever, except I wouldn't be able to see the darkness. I wouldn't even know that I was dead.

Years later, I saw a film about an insane man called What About Bob?, and the movie made me feel perfectly normal. There's this scene with a young boy about the age I was when I became obsessed with death. He's getting ready for bed one night and explains to Bob, portrayed by Bill Murray, that he's having an existential crisis, one very similar to what I went through.

This was the first time I encountered what I now believe to be a widespread terror. How widespread is unclear because many of us keep our darkest thoughts to ourselves, but our secret fears tend to leak out at the corners. It's evident in the way we talk about and respond to death.

Look at the bell contraptions installed in 18th and 19th century caskets to alert those above that a victim had been buried alive. Look at our obsession with ghosts, who return from the dead to haunt the living. Look at our religions, that promise us the sanctuary of eternal life. Look at the monsters we fear versus the ones we idolize.

Vampires are sexy because they never die. Sure, they have their quirks and torments, but they also have eternal youth. They are the lords of romance. Crisp clothes, worldly wisdom, a thing for necks. Vampires are the anti-death. Our fascination with them (our adulation, one might say), surely stems from their ability to defy our most primal fear: nonexistence.

The zombie on the other hand is not romanticized. This member of the undead offers the opposite allure of the vampire.

The zombie is in a permanent state of death.

And while some say the zombie dates to a particular film, like Romero's Night of the Living Dead or a book like Matheson's I am Legend, the truth is that our universal fear of death has sprinkled human history with many references to the same sort of beast. When we say that the first zombie film may have been Halperin's 1932 White Zombie, what they really mean is that this particular name for a universal creature first appeared in that film. But zombies are much older—they were just called something different.

In Europe, there were legends of rotting corpses walking around during the time of the Great Plague. In the Bible, Jesus returns from the dead and the buried rise from their graves and lumber about for a bit. The Haitian's had their own lore develop in the 19th century, and there's a history of zombie-like creatures popular in the Congo before that. You can go right back to one of the oldest stories ever told, the Epic of Gilgamesh, and find this reference:

I will knock down the Gates of the Netherworld,
I will smash the door posts, and leave the doors flat down,
and will let the dead go up to eat the living!
And the dead will outnumber the living!

When I wrote my own zombie book, told from the perspective of these enduring creatures, I was told that the timing was great, that they were newly popular. But zombies have been popular for as long as I can remember. What is quite possibly the most important music video of all time (certainly the one I watched more than any other) was a zombie flick with the King of Pop himself as one of the afflicted. And then there's the dozens of variations of Frankenstein being reanimated from the pieces of a corpse. Or the ghouls I saved (or sometimes didn't) in games like Fallout and Fallout 2.

Whether or not all of these are "real" zombies (and whether or not you believe some zombies are fast) is beside the point. What's fascinating is that the appeal is as old as time itself, and a bit of imagination might tell us why. Think of the state of primal man, how close people were to death. Bodies were something one dealt with personally. You didn't phone a professional, you took a loved one and disposed of the corpse. But all you know of bodies is that they get up and move around. Every morning we return from a state of suspended animation. So what do you think uncle Urg is going to do after you shovel some dirt over him? I'm guessing there were some unpleasant dreams in many a cave.

Beyond our fear of death, zombies present another series of primal disgusts. We evolved a distaste for putrescence as a survival mechanism. Human waste, pus, seeping wounds, gangrenous flesh, writhing maggots, swarming flies, these things wrinkle our nose just to read them (or write them!). There's good reason. We can get sick from these things. Rather than bother us on an intellectual and conscious level as to why we should back the hell up, nature just made us abhor such things. And when we concoct the ultimate evil, the perfect horror that is the walking dead, we coat them in all these disgusting fears as well.

There is no more perfect hate than that of a zombie. They are the compressed distillation of our many loathings. They are dread diamonds, the perfect monsters. And they have always been with us. Only the names have changed.

What do we love most about them? Killing them. Making their death permanent. Bashing that uniquely human frontal lobe, that part of us that feels most un-zombie, the seat of our supposed souls. If the reanimated dead seem to be gaining in popularity, it's only because we finally have the medium to do their stories justice. We have films and graphic novels; we have video games where scores of the foul beasts line up for our bullets. And we get to kill them over and over, unending waves of them, seeing how long we can fend them off, knowing, with the most perfect fear our brains can summon the same thing that little boy told Bill Murray:

"There's no way out of it. You're going to die. I'm going to die . . . What else is there to be afraid of?"

Of course, modern zombie tales have an answer for this question. There is something else to fear, something that speaks to a phobia that may not be deeper, but has become more widespread. It should be noted that the most horrific scenarios in many zombie tales are the cruel things human survivors do to one another. That's the post-apocalyptic side of the zombie story, the focus on the collapse of civilization and the subsequent rot of ethics and morality. But this is a new spin added to an old ghoul, and were it not for the presence of rotting, flesh-eating undead as far back as human literature reaches, it might be tempting to mistake this modern layer for a first cause.

But that would be just as bad as thinking the word "zombie" has anything to do with what the creatures represent. The Haitians of the 19th century would laugh. To them, a zombie may be harmless, just a person brought back from the dead, often to do the bidding of another. It is a word we adopted, a word that doesn't even appear in George A. Romero's first zombie film except in the credits. Words change. What we call our inner demons can be as fluid as language. But our descriptions of them, our fears of them, I believe they are eternal. We will always fear these representations of rot and death like no other creature we can summon. And they will not, I'll wager you anything, ever be seen as sexy. They sure as hell better not sparkle.

Hugh Howey author of "Wool" and "I Zombie"

PROLOGUE

The first sound to break the silence was almost unperceivable, a slight tug at the front door, which rippled across the room to punch fear through his heart.

Chaz Singleton jolted out of his chair and uncoiled like a Jack in the Box. He took a step, then froze in place to continue listening. More noises joined in, scattered across different points around the house...doors, windows and possibly the roof.

He was no longer alone.

They're here.

He turned a full circle, facing every wall, conveniently packaged in a split-level suburban house for them to tear away like gift wrapping. The predators had arrived with a single mission: To descend upon their prey.

One man versus...how many of them? Four? Eight? A dozen? More?

He glimpsed shadows gliding past the windows like ghosts. In the darkness of the house, they could not see him through the thin slits between curtains. It didn't matter. They sensed his presence. Their sounds grew more forceful and aggressive. The front door shook with a series of thuds. The window panes rattled.

He snatched up the baseball bat that leaned against the sofa. He gripped it hard but felt little comfort, recognizing its relative weakness against the strength and numbers of his enemy.

Fending off an attack was probably hopeless. Even if he stopped this mob, another would take its place. Hiding somewhere in the house was equally pointless. Every inch of space would be ripped apart until they found him.

Escape was the only option, relinquishing his home and all of its belongings to go on the run, plunging headfirst into a world where he would always be outnumbered, and a target.

As the pounding shook the walls, he shut his eyes and

reviewed the layout of the house. He needed to determine the exit with the least resistance and fewest pairs of hands waiting to grab him. He needed a clean path to vanish into the night.

Even if he escaped, then what?

His destination was uncertain, but he longed to find others like him and band together for safety. He feared such a search would prove fruitless. His only discovery might be the truth that he was the lone survivor of his race.

In a shockingly short period of time, everything in his world had been turned upside down and inside out. Instead of existing as one ordinary man among billions, he was now the outsider, the last representative of a rare species targeted for extinction.

He could no longer trust those who once befriended him...friends, neighbors and family. He was no longer one of them. They would view him in a brand new way. He posed a threat to their world...a bringer of doom. He hated what he had become, but it was never his choice.

Chaz Singleton, the last zombie on earth, stood alone, fighting for survival in a land of the living.

Shattering glass erupted across the room, accompanied by shouts, the entrance of intruders and the irresistible presence of sweaty, tasty flesh.

Chaz clenched his teeth and growled from somewhere deep within.

He planned his next move.

CHAPTER 1

Chaz Singleton awoke from the darkest, deepest sleep he had ever known, to find himself floating in a cloud of white: white ceiling, white floor, white walls, white pillow under his head and white sheets pulled up to his chin.

Numbness coated his body, creating a sensation of weightlessness. The surroundings confused him but also held a vague familiarity, like the soft edges of a faraway dream.

Chaz stirred his limbs. They felt heavy. His eyes winced in the light and his throat ached, thick and parched.

Where...am I?

He searched his memory and came up empty. If this was a hospital room, it was the ultimate in sterility without a hint of humanity or color. No phone, no television, no personal items or decorative touches of any kind.

Have I been sick...injured?

He clawed through the cobwebs in his mind.

Kelly. Where was Kelly? He tried to speak his wife's name but his voice only croaked, a foreign instrument, unused for how long?

How long have I been...here?

He remembered...fajitas. Dinner at his favorite Mexican restaurant at the mall with Kelly. They had gone there after running an errand at the sporting goods store. He needed running shoes. There was a sale...or they had a coupon. Kelly was interested in the treadmills. They talked to a salesman who was eager to sell the latest model...but Chaz backed off after hearing the price...and then he shot some free throws at the basketball net on display. Then came the fajitas, a margarita, followed by the trip back home. He watched part of a hockey game. Then...

Up early the next morning for work at a new construction site, the extension of a strip mall in Tucson. He had to operate the crane...lifting and transporting drywall materials over a wall and into a roofless structure where a bank branch would one day blossom.

And there the memories stopped.

Simple and unremarkable. Shopping and dinner with Kelly, some television, an early rise, followed by another construction gig with the crew. Mike... Louie... Carlos... Ted.

He was pleased to remember the names and recall faces. The fog was lifting.

But just enough remained to obscure why he was here. And where was *here*?

"Kel-ley," he said, a stuttering whisper, his voice sounding strange in his ears. He tried to swallow but there was nothing to swallow.

His entire being felt covered by one big, dull ache, a second skin stretched too tight. His stomach swam with a strange hunger.

He barely felt connected to his arms and legs, but when he shifted under the sheets, they moved with him, obedient to his commands.

"Kelly," he said, stronger, almost a real voice breaking through.

He thought hard. Have I been in a car wreck? Did I have a heart attack? Did something happen at work or at home? If I've been in a coma...why aren't I hooked up to anything? I'm just laying here...like a slab.

"*Kelly*," he said firmly. No one answered. He was alone. Where was his wife? Had she been visiting? Did she even know he was here?

He felt his head clearing. He turned his focus to getting out of the bed. He would hunt down some answers. Clearly the answers were not going to come to him.

Across the room, he could see a door, white of course, closed securely to blend into the wall, leaving only its outline with a handle.

Chaz wanted to know what he would find beyond that door.

He sat up.

His body jerked, lurching in a clumsy motion. He swayed like a toddler fighting for balance.

He felt a momentary rush of dizziness, waited for it to clear, then started his next action, pushing away the sheets.

He wore a simple white gown, something a hospital patient would wear, which furthered his suspicions that he had suffered some kind of terrible accident.

But what? He wasn't bandaged. There wasn't any particular part of him that felt worse than any other...just the overall sluggishness. All body parts accounted for.

He swung his legs over the side of the bed. The gown flapped to reveal the grayish blue color of his thighs. The marble-like hue contrasted sharply with the white sheets.

Oh my God, I AM sick, he realized, and stared at his arms, which held the same disturbing color. Looking more closely, it wasn't so much a color as it was a lack of color, as if blood no longer moved through his veins.

"Kelly!" he shouted with a punch of air, loud and afraid. He slid off the bed, his feet thudding to the floor. He threw his hands out for balance as the room spun in immediate response to his sudden movement.

As he lurched into his first step away from the bed, a loud, electronic beeping erupted, the first noise of any kind from his environment. He fell back against the bed as the electronic beeps continued to fill his ears.

The door at the other end of the room opened and a man rushed forward, bald with a gray beard, large glasses and a white lab coat.

Like the room, he looked vaguely familiar; someone previously glimpsed but not comprehended.

"Steady," said the man as he reached Chaz.

Chaz dropped back against the bed, stammering his way through a complete sentence. "Where—where—where am I?"

The bald man pulled a remote-like device from his pocket and jabbed it with his thumb to stop the pulsing alarm.

The room fell silent. The bald man studied Chaz for a long moment as if he was trying to look inside his head.

"Chaz Singleton?" he said.

Chaz hesitated, then nodded.

"Can you speak?"

Chaz said, "Yes," and the reply appeared to startle, then please the man. He asked his next question.

"So you know who you are?"

"Of course," said Chaz.

"Where do you live?"

"337 Kelton Lane, Tucson."

"Your age?"

"Forty-eight."

"Occupation?"

"I'm a construction worker. Why?"

"Recite the alphabet."

"Are you kidding me?"

"Please."

Chaz did so. Then he asked, "What is this about? Where am I? Who are you?"

"My name is Dr. Rabe," said the man. "You've had a very bad accident. Do you remember any of it?"

Chaz thought hard and had to shake his head. "No. I must have amnesia. What kind of accident?"

"What's the last thing you remember?" asked Dr. Rabe, maintaining his calm, steady voice.

"I woke up early. I went to work. We're building an extension to the shopping strip on Grayhawk Drive. I was operating the crane to move roofing materials. Did something happen?"

Dr. Rabe said, "You were electrocuted."

Chaz let the word sink in for a moment. "Electrocuted?"

"Your crane tipped over. The top of the crane struck a power line. You were electrocuted. Others were hurt, but you...you took the brunt of it. How do you feel?"

"Very stiff."

"Anything else?"

"Tired. Confused. How long have I been asleep?"

"Physically or mentally?" asked Dr. Rabe.

The question gave Chaz pause. "What do you mean?"

Dr. Rabe said, "You've been up and about for two weeks."

"I don't remember it. Only the faintest memories..."

"Your mind was in a primal state," said Dr. Rabe. "You only existed at the most basic level. Walking. Grasping at things.

6

Eating."

The word "eating" triggered a realization in Chaz. "I'm starved," he said. "I'm really, really hungry. My stomach feels like it's on fire."

"Yes, of course. We shall take care of that immediately," said Dr. Rabe with a touch of nervousness that Chaz found odd. "Please remain where you are."

Dr. Rabe walked across the room and opened the door to a small, white refrigerator, nearly indistinguishable from the white cabinets on either side. He returned to Chaz with a pink Tupperware container and a fork.

Dr. Rabe peeled back the lid on the container. Chaz looked inside.

"What is it? Lasagna?" he asked.

Dr. Rabe simply smiled and offered him a fork. "Not quite."

"Doesn't smell like anything."

"You've lost your sense of smell. Go ahead."

Chaz accepted the pink container and fork. He started to dig in.

His sluggish body suddenly sparkled with sensations.

"Oh my God," said Chaz. "This is delicious."

"I was afraid you'd say that," muttered Dr. Rabe, more to himself than Chaz. He watched with a frown as Chaz quickly devoured the meal.

Chaz licked the Tupperware clean. He startled himself with the impulsive behavior. "I must have been famished. When's the last time I ate?"

"This morning," said Dr. Rabe, taking the container and fork from him and putting them aside.

The feeding gave Chaz a fresh burst of strength and energy. His mind felt sharper. More than anything, he was ready to leave the trappings of the four white walls and reunite with Kelly.

"I need to see my wife. Where is she?"

Dr. Rabe stared down at the floor. "I'm afraid you can't see her right now. Perhaps you should get some more rest."

"I feel better. I don't need any more rest. Where is Kelly? I'd like to leave."

Dr. Rabe looked back up at him, squarely in the eye. "I'm

sorry, Chaz. You can't leave. You are required to stay here with us."

"What is here? Who is us?" Chaz took a step toward Dr. Rabe, feeling a rise of anger. The entire situation felt very strange and claustrophobic. He wanted out. "Tell me."

"Now is not the time," said Dr. Rabe, not budging from his path.

"You can't keep me here against my will!"

Chaz gave Dr. Rabe a sudden shove, pushing him to one side. He advanced several steps before Rabe pulled out the remote from his pocket and pressed a button.

Almost instantly, two large men in combat fatigues entered the room. One of them carried shackles.

Chaz froze. "What the hell is this? What is going on? *Who are you people?"*

"All in good time," said Dr. Rabe calmly.

Chaz made a run for the door but the two large men pounced on him and knocked him to the floor. They cuffed his wrists and ankles and then brought out a strange leather muzzle. They forced his head back and secured it around his mouth, tightly, like a gag. Chaz struggled but his movements were limited by the shackles. He lay on the floor, bound like a prisoner. The three men stared down at him, cold and stoic.

Chaz screamed into the muzzle and his words became trapped in a thick, muffled roar.

"Who are you? Where is my wife? What is happening to me?"

CHAPTER 2

Chaz spent the next two days in a ten-by-ten, windowless jail cell so pristine that it appeared to have been created just for him. He had a bed, essentially a mattress and sheet, but he didn't sleep much. He had a toilet but no urges to use it, despite a steady diet of the strange but sublime lasagna delivered through the narrow opening across his cell's steel bars.

On many occasions, during long stretches of isolation, he grabbed those bars and screamed for explanations.

He wanted to see his wife.

He wanted to talk with his son, Peter, a student at Columbia University in New York.

Did they know where he was? And where were they?

Overall, he felt like hell. His total being retained one big, creeping ache that he could not shake, like a relentless flu. His mood swings alarmed him not for their outbursts of anger and sorrow, but for the longer periods where he felt nothing at all, as if his emotions had been rubbed away.

Dr. Rabe came by several times each day, calm and soft spoken, but always accompanied by overgrown thugs in military fatigues to thwart any attempts at escape. Every morning Rabe rolled a cart of medical equipment into the cell and subjected Chaz to a battery of tests, many of them involving big syringes that oddly caused no pain.

Chaz bombarded Rabe with questions, the same ones, over and over like a broken record. The answers remained vague but always hinted at more information to come "when the time is right."

"I want to know now!" demanded Chaz to no avail.

At one point, bursting with frustration, he lunged at Rabe, intending to grab him by the lab coat and shake answers out of him. The big goons tackled Chaz before he could land a hand. In swift coordination, they shackled his arms and legs and then wrapped his face in a muzzle, as if he was a rabid Rottweiler.

9

The brown leather mask covered his nose and mouth with small punctured openings so he could breathe. It was secured tight in the back with straps. They left it on until he settled down and Rabe signaled to remove it.

"What was that all about? Do you think I'm going to bite you?" he asked Rabe with sharp sarcasm.

Rabe didn't reply.

Then one day—or was it night, there was no way of telling— the cell opened, the goons shackled his wrists and ankles and Rabe announced they were going to visit someone important.

Rabe spoke the name with a tone of reverence: Breck Palmer.

"Who the hell is Breck Palmer?" asked Chaz.

"You'll find out soon enough" came Rabe's predictable reply.

Shuffling in shackles, Chaz advanced down a long, dim corridor with Dr. Rabe, followed by two armed thugs in green fatigues.

As they rounded a corner, Chaz heard a low, eerie moaning. The noise became a thicket of murmuring voices spiked with animal-like grunts and growls. With every step, the sounds grew louder and more distinct, bouncing off the bare walls like dancing spirits.

They rounded another corner and Chaz encountered a cage of deranged faces pressed against steel bars, arms extended and clawing at air. Draped in dirty, torn clothing, the mob pushed and shoved one another with sluggish aggression, as if doped up.

As they caught sight of Chaz and his escorts, their cries grew frantic, an eruption of barks and shrieks. Rabe said, "Don't look at them," but Chaz couldn't tear his eyes away.

Like a throng of entangled mental patients, they pulsed as one entity, slack jawed and staring out with lost, deadened eyes.

These prisoners displayed the same rough skin and jerky mobility that Chaz experienced, but they were not clear-headed beings pleading for understanding. They behaved like a pack of hungry, confused animals.

Rabe led Chaz further down the corridor. The moans and shrieks faded, but Chaz couldn't shake the ugly noises out of his head.

Finally the foursome arrived at a small network of

windowless offices guarded by a soldier with a rifle. The soldier recognized Dr. Rabe and nodded.

Rabe brought Chaz into the tidy, compact office of Breck Palmer.

Palmer rose from his chair. He was younger than Rabe but definitely the man in charge, wearing a dark suit with dark hair slicked back and a hint of gray at the temples. His eyes showed no warmth, just an intense focus, as if he was constantly studying everything around him.

One of Rabe's escorts said, "We'll be just outside the door if you need us" and departed with his partner.

The door shut.

Palmer studied Chaz. Chaz remained silent.

"Mr. Palmer," said Dr. Rabe with a touch of pride in his voice, "I'd like you to meet Chaz Singleton."

"Hello, Chaz" said Palmer in a flat voice. He did not offer his hand.

"Hello," said Chaz.

The simple response caused Palmer to raise his eyebrows. He broke out in a smile. He leaned back in his chair while Rabe and Chaz remained standing.

"Chaz," said Palmer. "On my desk, there is a black pen. Do you see it?"

Chaz nodded.

"I command you to pick it up."

Chaz looked at Palmer with a look of suspicion and puzzlement. "Why?"

"Because I have said for you to do so." He then repeated the request in a staccato tone, as if speaking to a dog. "Pick-up-the-pen."

Chaz replied, "No."

Palmer frowned. He folded his arms.

"Chaz," said Palmer. "Tell me. What are you thinking right now?"

Chaz hesitated, then spoke exactly what was on his mind, no holds barred. "I want to know who the hell you are. I want to know why I am here. I want to see my family. You cannot hold me here against my will. I don't know how I became your guinea pig, but I won't stand for it. Something terrible is going on here. I don't know who or what is in that cage, but it can't be legal. I have the right to know what's going on and to be set free."

Chaz stopped talking, ready for a response.

Instead, he received silence. He noticed Rabe was smiling...actually beaming as if Chaz had just delivered a Pulitzer Prize winning speech rather than a simple plea for explanation and freedom.

"Very, very interesting," said Palmer.

"He's intelligent," said Rabe. "Articulate. Forceful."

"Yes," said Palmer, and then he sighed. "But what good is that... if he can't be obedient?"

"What do you mean, sir?"

"With intelligence comes free will."

Rabe said, "But without intelligence, we get...we get..." and he gestured with a waving hand to the corridor from where they came. "We get *them*."

Palmer stood up. He circled his desk to go toe to toe with Chaz. He looked him over, then gave him a sudden poke in the ribs.

Chaz didn't react. He was surprised he didn't at least flinch in reflex.

"He smells as bad as the others," said Palmer. "His appearance is already affected."

"We haven't been able to reverse that yet, sir," said Rabe.

"It's good progress," said Palmer, but it clearly wasn't the praise Rabe expected. "Keep it up. Now please remove him before the odor makes me vomit."

Chaz stared hard at Palmer. "I don't know who you are," he said, "but *fuck you*."

Chaz reached out, grabbed the black pen off his desk and snapped it in two. He tossed the pieces to the floor.

"Therein lies the problem," said Palmer. He turned his back on Rabe and Chaz. He returned to the big chair behind his desk without another word.

Rabe and Chaz departed from Palmer's office. Rabe looked distraught. The two armed escorts stepped forward to join them on the walk back to Chaz's cell.

"I'll be fine," said Rabe. "He's shackled. He's not going anywhere."

The two guards looked at one another, then stepped back to let them go.

"Come with me," said Rabe to Chaz. He stared back at Palmer's office with a look of hurt and disgust. "You know how I keep saying I'll tell you what's happening when the time is right?"

Chaz nodded.

"Well the time is right." Rabe lowered his voice as they walked. "We're going to turn into one of the small storage rooms up ahead. I'm going to tell you the purpose of this lab and why you are the way you are. You need to know."

When they reached the storage room door, Chaz stopped. He faced Rabe. "Before we go in, tell me one thing," said Chaz. "Am I ever getting out of here alive?"

Rabe almost smiled.

"I'm afraid that's not possible," he replied, "because you are already dead."

CHAPTER 3

Dr. Rabe escorted Chaz into the small storage room of lab supplies and shut the door.

The room contained stacks of boxes, a humming fluorescent light and, like every other space Chaz had seen since awakening from his coma, no windows. The outside world did not exist. They could be anywhere. At the same time, it felt like nowhere, a sparsely populated bunker without a climate or any indication of day or night. They could be on the moon for all he knew.

Chaz sat on one of the boxes, prepared for another weird, cagey conversation of elusive explanations. Dr. Rabe remained standing, biting his lower lip until he could no longer suppress the words and they tumbled out in a frantic spill.

"I'm going to tell you some things that you were not meant to know. If you repeat any of this to anyone we'll both be destroyed. Do you understand?"

Chaz nodded. "Understood."

"We are in a top secret, underground, biomedical research lab of scientists and doctors conducting experiments on behalf of the department of defense. The man you just met, Breck Palmer, is the leader of this organization and our conduit back to the government agency that funds our research. The holding pen you saw with the people who looked like they were sleepwalking...those are some of our experiments."

Chaz frowned. "I would have to say your experiments don't look like much of a success."

"A success? Yes and no."

"How could you call those things a success? They're barely alive."

"Mr. Singleton, it's a miracle they're alive at all. They used to be dead."

Chaz pondered this, then grinned. "No. That's ridiculous. I don't believe it."

"Those individuals have been reanimated from the dead. They are proof it can be done. And *you* are proof."

Chaz immediately lost his grin.

Rabe continued. "Chaz Singleton, you died on Thursday, April the second. As far as the rest of the world is concerned...you are dead and buried in Tucson Memorial Cemetery."

Chaz shook his head. "You're crazy. I think I would know if I was dead."

"You were dead for six days."

"Impossible. You're playing mind games with me. I'm beginning to think this is some kind of psychological test. Where are the cameras?"

Rabe continued in the same steady tone. "That construction accident took your life. You were hit with 9,000 volts of electricity. It killed you instantly. Your heart stopped beating. Your breathing stopped. One of your coworkers tried CPR. The paramedics tried to resuscitate you with a defibrillator. They did everything they could but they couldn't save you. You were pronounced dead at the scene. It made the local news. You had a wake. You had a funeral. Your wife, son, friends, coworkers and neighbors all watched as your coffin was lowered into the ground. But you weren't in it. We intercepted your body in the dead of night. We have been waiting for a specimen like you. Young, freshly deceased, in excellent shape with your internal organs undamaged and intact. You were brought to this facility deep in the desert, out of sight and undetected by any map or GPS. Technically, this lab does not exist. We have a highly classified mission that must not be compromised. It's a matter of national security. We call it Operation Invincible. We're committed to building the army of the future."

"Army of the future?" said Chaz, incredulous. "You mean those...those things?"

"Call it a work in progress."

"I don't know what to call it."

"It's a critical first step. Think about it. What's the biggest flaw of any army? Vulnerability. Mortality. Soldiers die, often in big numbers. But what if you established a fighting force that could not be killed...because they were already dead. There's no threat to the living...no public outcry about combat missions…no military payroll or pensions funded by taxpayers. In short, nothing to lose on the road to victory."

"So you send corpses to war...rather than sending corpses home from war."

"Yes," said Dr. Rabe. "A zombie army. Cold, relentless, fighting machines. We set out to revive the recently dead. After a long period of experimentation, we were finally successful. Where we failed was mind control. We created dozens of zombies, but they were useless. You saw the results. They are clumsy, stupid, brain dead. We couldn't get them to do what we wanted. Their minds were too primitive, operating only on the most basic instincts, unable to effectively use weapons or discern the good from the bad." Rabe gestured to Chaz. "But then we had a new breakthrough. We took the experiment one step forward. I developed a stimulant to reactivate the brain to something resembling its former self. You are my prize, the first of a new breed. A 'smart zombie.'"

Chaz took it all in, stunned. "So am I dead or alive?"

"Neither and both."

"What makes you think I'm going to enlist in your zombie army?"

Rabe sighed. "We've already contemplated that. You're smarter than the other zombies. But you're too smart. That's why Breck Palmer was testing you, seeing if you would follow orders. But it appears as though you've retained a mind of your own."

"That's a good thing, isn't it?"

"I suppose."

"Then why not let me go?"

"Let you go?" Dr. Rabe stared at him as if the notion was unthinkable. "Oh no, no, no. We gave you life. Now you belong to us."

"When can I see my wife and son? How long are you going to hold me here?"

"I'm afraid I can't answer that."

"Why not?"

"We need to learn more about how you exist, your abilities

and potential. Our research has only just begun. You are the first of a new race."

"You can't hold me here forever."

"You think you could fit back into normal society? And go back to the way everything was?"

"Why not?"

"You might be resurrected from the dead, but you're not the same person. You can never be the same. For one thing, you..." Then Rabe stopped and sighed. "Maybe it's best you see for yourself."

Rabe escorted Chaz out of the conference room and they returned to the long, dim corridor. They reached a door simply marked Restroom.

Rabe opened the door.

"Should I be afraid?" asked Chaz.

Rabe didn't answer and gestured for Chaz to enter.

Chaz stepped into the small bathroom. He came face to face with a sickly looking man with bluish skin, gray teeth and sunken eyes. Chaz gasped twice—once for the frightful image that startled him, and then a second time upon the realization that this was his own reflection.

Chaz stared into a large mirror overlooking the sink.

"Dear God, what happened to me?"

"You died. We can't undo what that does to one's physical appearance. Each day, it gets a little worse as you decompose."

"I look horrible," Chaz said. "I look like I shouldn't even be standing."

"But you are. That's the miracle."

"Some miracle."

Chaz felt overwhelmed by sudden dizziness. He turned away from the mirror and bent forward, hands on knees. "I don't feel so good."

"You're probably hungry. It's been a while since you ate."

Dr. Rabe led him back into the corridor. "Come. We need to get you to your cell before someone notices you're still missing. You're a very important specimen here. Your absence will be noted."

Rabe led Chaz down the winding path. Chaz walked in short

steps with his ankles shackled to prevent him from breaking into a run. Even if he could run, Chaz had no clue where he would find an exit.

They walked back past the large holding cell packed with "dumb zombies." The prisoners groaned, shuffled and stared out with dark, mournful eyes. Chaz realized he looked just like these pitiful creatures...a member of the blue skins. He was closer to their race than the race of the living and healthy.

"You were like that for several weeks," said Rabe, "until I discovered the right serum to reanimate your brain to something like its original function. Soon, we will do the same for another specimen, a young woman named Dolores. She died from an allergic reaction that caused her throat to swell shut. Otherwise, she's in great shape, like you."

"So I won't be the only one?"

"There will be others. My work will continue. This is just the start. I will rename the two of you Adam and Eve. The beginning of a new breed."

Chaz started to buckle again. Hunger consumed him.

"I need to eat..."

"Of course. Come this way." Rabe led him into a room with a large, stainless steel meat freezer. He retrieved a purple Tupperware container and Chaz felt a surge of energy and excitement, like a starving dog presented with a juicy steak.

He loved this food.

He ate the same thing every day, twice a day.

And he had no idea what it was.

Rabe had barely presented the container to him before Chaz threw off the lid and started digging in with his fingers. He scooped the red and pink gobs into his mouth, no time for fussing with utensils. This food needed a fast and direct trip down the gullet.

He stuffed himself crazy, then belched.

Chaz put the container down. He looked at the floor. He felt silly about his behavior.

"So...this is part of my 'undead' state? I eat like a pig?"

"Yes, but as you have seen, your diet is somewhat limited."

"All you feed me is this weird lasagna shit."

"You wouldn't eat anything else if I offered it."

"Are you sure?"

"We've run tests. You are not capable of digesting most foods and liquids. You have very restricted eating habits. This is what worries us most. It could jeopardize the entire experiment and shut us down unless we find a cure."

"A cure?" said Chaz. "A cure for what?"

"Your uncontrollable appetite for human flesh."

Chaz stared back at Rabe in horror but couldn't challenge the statement, because deep down he knew it was true. It explained the strange urges that haunted him every day since awakening from his coma, the awful craving that made no sense but now received an official validation.

He desired to bite every living human being he encountered. He wanted to sink his teeth into them and gobble down big, bloody chunks.

"The only thing that has prevented you from chewing off my face is the meal of human flesh I feed you twice a day," said Dr. Rabe.

Chaz could only say, "But...why?"

"We continue to research this strange anomaly. Somehow ingesting the flesh of the living rejuvenates your own dead tissue, like a leech feeding off the blood of others."

"What about those things in the cage," said Chaz. "Are they..."

"They're the same way. All of you are. With no discretion over whom you bite."

Chaz lowered his head. He shut his eyes at the madness. "Then you better lock me up," he said, feeling a small gurgle deep in his stomach and yearning for the pale, soft skin of Dr. Rabe's throat. "Because I'm still hungry."

CHAPTER 4

A gunshot boomed from somewhere deep in the maze of corridors, echoing off the walls in a crazy ricochet. Chaz leapt across the cell and threw himself against the bars. He craned his neck but could only glimpse a short distance of empty white tunnel.

Another gunshot followed, then several more in rapid succession accompanied by distant, distorted shouts. The cacophony of gunfire quickly grew dense, filling Chaz's ears like the finale to a fourth of July fireworks display.

Dr. Rabe ran toward the cell, his long lab coat flapping behind him.

"What's happening?" said Chaz.

Hands shaking, Rabe produced a key and unlocked the cell door. Typically, Rabe visited in the accompaniment of one or more armed guards. This time he was solo and lit up with panic.

"They're—they're shutting down the operation." Rabe entered the cell, out of breath.

"Shutting it down?"

"They're destroying the zombies." Dr. Rabe saw the immediate look of fear in Chaz's eyes and clarified: "The dumb zombies. The ones in the holding pen. They're doing away with all of them."

"But what about me?"

"I told them to spare you," said Rabe. His voice wavered, not exactly confident. "You're not like the others. You're special. You can think, feel, reason..."

"I'm nothing like the others!"

"Of course not. I told Breck—"

"You told me to save your friend the 'smart' zombie," said Breck Palmer, now standing outside the cell, accompanied by two armed soldiers. "You were proud of your dead carcass with a thinking brain."

Dr. Rabe spun around, terrified. Palmer moved his gaze to Chaz. "So I presume you have heard the news, Mr. Singleton. Or should I say, the former Mr. Singleton. The real Mr. Singleton died in a construction accident three weeks ago. You are the reanimated corpse of someone whose soul has left this earth, a military experiment of good intentions gone horribly awry."

The echo of gunshots continued to travel through distant corridors.

"You're shutting down the operation," said Chaz.

"Yes," said Palmer. "You heard correctly. The orders come from high above. We are aborting this project. My daily reports became increasingly worrisome to our sponsors. Let's just say this work is too controversial to take forward. There would be an enormous public outcry if word of a zombie lab ever got out. The moral issues of playing God at the taxpayer's expense would surely bring down the current administration with a tough election year ahead. The risks aren't worth the reward. We wanted to create a viable army for the future. All we did was create a bunch of lumbering idiots that don't know up from down."

"But what about me?" said Chaz. "What about Dr. Rabe's advances to reactivate the brain? You can create a higher form of reanimated life. You can still turn this into something good."

Dr. Rabe stayed silent in anticipation of Palmer's firm rebuttal.

"We can't turn you loose into society. Let's be realistic. You may be advanced compared to those drooling creatures down the hall but a fatal flaw persists. Don't tell me you don't know what I'm talking about. The sickness."

"The sickness?"

"The hunger," said Palmer. More gunshots rang out, getting closer. Palmer continued speaking in a flat monotone, undisturbed by the carnage in the background. "You and the other beasts can only survive on the flesh of the living. It's the basic instinct of every zombie and highly contagious. When a member of the living is bitten, they become infected, turn stupid and the virus spreads. Another zombie is born. If we continued, we might unleash a pandemic that would be impossible to contain. We couldn't give everyone the same advanced treatment you received. The reality is that the 'dumb zombie' population would spread like wildfire and destroy civilization as we know it. The purpose of this mission was to create a new breed of soldier to carry out military actions without causalities. You can't kill something that's already dead. Unfortunately, you also cannot control the dead and their strange appetite for the living. You can't have the servants attacking their masters, Chaz Singleton. This operation is over. We are erasing any evidence it even existed. We own the creations and their destiny. The zombies are being deactivated. We will seal up this lab and destroy it."

Rabe gasped. "All of my research, my serums, the equipment...?"

"Yes," said Palmer. "Not a trace will remain. Not the lab. Not the experiments. And, I am sorry to say, not the medical staff."

Rabe's eyes grew wide with fear. "You can't possibly mean..."

"Please, understand," said Palmer. "This is in the interests of national security. We are only doing our patriotic duty."

In a brisk, mechanical movement, one of the guards fired on Rabe, ripping a fatal hole through his chest. The other guard aimed his rifle for Chaz's face—blasting one second too late as Chaz jerked to the side and a bullet tore past his cheek.

Rabe crumpled to the ground and Chaz roared forward, crashing into the men before they could steady their weapons for additional shots. He felt an unnatural animal ferocity, three days of being caged, many more lost to a zombie haze, now replaced by a huge surge of strength.

Chaz burned with one goal: Escape.

He grabbed the two guards and slammed them together like cymbals, hearing their heads collide in a grotesque crunch. He saved the biggest blow for Breck Palmer, pounding him in the mouth with such force that the smarmy, suit-wearing prick flew backwards into the cell bars, striking them with a long, extended KLANGGG.

Chaz surprised himself with his superhuman strength, more than he ever possessed while alive, even as a well-fit, six-foot-two construction worker. He realized the numbness that dismissed pain also pumped him with a heightened sense of physical power.

When one of the guards fired a bullet at Chaz from the floor, it sliced through the top of his shoulder. He saw the spray of his own blood but felt no impact or disablement, only increased fury. He kicked the guard with a crushing strike to the skull and the loud groan in response signaled that this member of the living experienced the full range of pain.

Chaz dashed across the tangled, bloodied men at his feet and escaped through the open cell door. He promptly spun around and slammed the door shut, Dr. Rabe's key still protruding from the lock. He twisted it, heard a click, and flung the key down the corridor, where it hit the white tile floor and skidded far out of reach.

"I'll get you, you blue-skinned bastard!" shouted Palmer through bloody lips, rising to his knees, no longer tidy and controlled but disheveled and shaking with rage. A battered guard staggered to his feet and aimed his weapon through the cell bars.

Chaz ran off and a spray of bullets tore up the wall where he had just been standing.

Chaz remembered some of the twists and turns in the long, underground corridors from his trip to Palmer's office, but he had no real guess for where an exit might exist. He knew he was running straight into the sounds of slaughter.

To fuel his perseverance, he fixated on his wife Kelly and son Peter. He wanted to see them again. He wanted to hold them in a tight embrace and declare to the world: *I am not dead.*

The sounds of gunfire, shouts of soldiers and falling bodies grew louder with every step. Chaz turned a corner and skidded into a nest of chaos. A half dozen men in military fatigues stood in a firm row, wrapped in guns and ammunition, spraying bullets into the open door of the zombie holding pen. Dead zombies littered the ground, an oxymoron on display, decommissioned corpses piled up like bloody, stuffed laundry. The creatures that remained on their feet staggered in circles, tripping over their colleagues, groaning when bullets hit, but making no real attempt to escape or fight back.

The armed men clearly enjoyed this activity, laughing out loud with each hit. Many of the zombies required multiple shots to bring them down and twirled like comical sprinklers of blood.

"In the head!" shouted one of the men.

Chaz knew he had to make a mad dash through this firing squad, which meant being seen, which meant being shot at. He braced himself and roared forward.

"Hey, one got loose!" shouted a guard.

Chaz created fists and stretched out his arms like battering rams, smashing into the startled soldiers before they could swivel their weapons in his direction. Clearly, they had not experienced a zombie that fought back with speed and precision.

The other zombies grunted excitedly like roused primates, energized by his defiance.

"Run, you idiots!" Chaz yelled at them, but they seemed more interested in watching the proceedings than grabbing control of their own destinies.

Bullets pounded the floor and walls around Chaz. He reached the other side of the corridor, thankful to still be on his feet and marveling over his escape from the heavy artillery.

He ran another fifty feet through the tunnel, whipping around several turns, glimpsing blurred faces unprepared for a running blue skin. When he reached a split in directions, he stopped for a moment and studied his alternatives: two identical, long, white corridors.

That's when he realized he hadn't escaped the gunfire entirely unharmed. He noticed a red bullet hole just below his left ribs...and then another in his right thigh.

Holy shit.

His instincts told him to collapse to the floor but he stood there just fine, feeling no pain, just a slight, irritating itch, like a couple of splinters needing to be tweezed.

What the hell?

The crack of a rifle rang out behind him.

No time to contemplate, *what the hell?* He had to continue his desperate dash for freedom.

Chaz picked a corridor and ran.

He realized he was running toward a new battlefield of gunshots and commotion, although this one had an alarming difference—the screams of living humans replacing the groans and oophs of bewildered zombies.

Chaz turned a corner and caught a full view of one of the large laboratories. Armed guards in military fatigues blocked the opening, their backs to Chaz, continuing their slaughter, this time targeting the medical staff. Terrified doctors and researchers scampered for shelter behind tables of test tubes, beakers and computer equipment. The gunfire sent glass exploding in all directions and stained the white lab coats red.

"Why are you doing this?" screamed an elderly doctor, before a shot to the throat shut him up and he fell against a rack of medical utensils.

Chaz couldn't believe his eyes. Palmer's men were clearly conducting a clean sweep to eradicate any and all evidence of the zombie experiment. Innocent men and women were being massacred alongside the sleepwalking dead.

One of the doctors, a freckled young man with an arm oozing blood, slipped through the barricade of armed guards and entered the corridor, stopping for a fearful moment in front of Chaz.

"It's okay," said Chaz. "I'll help you."

Two of the guards spun around to confront the escapee—and faced the additional challenge of Chaz.

Chaz surprised them with an abrupt attack, lunging forward and pounding with his fists. He grabbed one guard by the collar of his shirt, lifted him off the ground like a small child and threw him head first into two other guards. Bodies toppled like bowling pins.

"Run!" Chaz barked at the freckled young doctor.

Chaz and the doctor dashed down the corridor. Chaz slowed his pace to let the doctor take the lead.

"Do you know the way to the exit?" asked Chaz.

"Yes," came the response. "Follow me."

They weaved through a maze of tunnels as shots and shouts continued to echo in surround sound around them. They crossed a section of corridor littered with more dead zombies, each one leaking from a gaping head wound. Chaz started to slip on a huge puddle of blood and fought to prevent himself from falling to the ground.

"We're almost there," said the freckled doctor, gasping.

The corridor widened into a small lobby-like area with a man at a desk backed by two armed soldiers with hands resting on powerful assault rifles.

"Go for the door," said Chaz. "I'll bring down the guards."

His words alerted the soldiers. By the time they had turned toward Chaz, he was flying at them.

Raging like a rabid animal, Chaz attacked.

The freckled doctor grabbed the door handle and pulled—but it didn't budge.

"We're locked in!" he screamed, spinning around in panic.

"Move away from the door!" shouted Chaz. He held one of the high-powered rifles he snatched from a guard who now lay unconscious on the floor.

The doctor dove out of the way and Chaz blasted the door with a continuous round of firepower, exploding glass and bending metal until the door flopped from its hinges.

"*GO!*" screamed Chaz.

The doctor advanced through the door, successfully squeezing past a gap opened up by the assault weapon's barrage.

Chaz had neutralized the two guards but the chubby man behind the desk, while unarmed by weapons, was equipped with something even more powerful—an alarm.

He pounced on a small switch and the entire bunker ignited with a blast of pulsing, electronic shrieks.

Chaz punched the chubby man to the floor but the damage was done, and he knew more soldiers would soon flood the lobby.

There was no time to lose.

Chaz threw himself against the broken door and its remaining pieces came apart, allowing him to spill outdoors. The bright, natural light startled him—a sensation he had not experienced in nearly a month.

The outside world flooded him with hope, evidence that reality still existed. The bunker was not some endless nightmare but an isolated slice of Hell on earth. The sweeping desert winds replaced the stale bunker air and invigorated him with life.

Freedom at last.

The freckled doctor ran down a thin path to a small parking lot of cars. Chaz followed him.

He saw a bland, innocuous sign near the bunker entrance, "Botanical Research Laboratories," clearly a misleading front for the horrors within. The size of the building was very small, concealing the fact that it incorporated a much bigger underground network of facilities.

"Thank God, thank God, thank God!" exclaimed the young doctor as he reached his car, a blue Nissan. He dug for his keys and a single shot rang out. The doctor fell dead to the gravel, a bullet hole torn through his back and into his heart.

Chaz whipped around to find the source of the gunfire and saw a sniper on the building's roof, dressed in black, wearing a black cap and poised for the next shot.

Breck Palmer's hit men had every escape route covered, including the parking lot for any lucky survivors who made it that far.

Crack! A bullet bit into the ground at Chaz's feet. He jumped and then a second one struck him in the chest.

Chaz gasped, started to fall back, but then sprang forward, a reflex of defiance. He realized the pain and injury was all in his mind—these gun wounds, like the others, were an isolated flare of irritation, but nothing that would bring him down.

Chaz jumped away from the fallen doctor's car. More sniper fire pounded the ground, throwing dirt and gravel. Bullets sprayed the side of the Nissan with small black holes and blew out the back window.

Chaz circled to the other side of the car, using it for cover. The bullets continued to rain down on him. He heard more shouts and discovered additional armed soldiers emerging from the building, weapons drawn.

Shit!

Chaz raced through the rows of parked cars, remaining just a few footsteps ahead of the staccato blast of bullets striking the earth behind him.

Chaz reached an SUV with a huge spider-web crack across the windshield on the driver's side. He peered inside and found a gray-haired man in a lab coat sitting behind the wheel, a bullet hole in his forehead and dribbling a steady flow of blood.

Another near escape, stopped by the sniper.

Chaz began to turn away, then spun back, realizing the significance of a small flash of reflection in the front seat.

Car keys in the ignition.

"Surround him!" hollered a commanding voice, as soldiers continued to spill from the lab entrance. They swarmed the parking lot and formed a tightening circle around Chaz and the SUV.

Chaz climbed into the vehicle. He grabbed the dead driver and pushed him aside.

Gunfire pounded the SUV, bursting the side windows.

Chaz started up the car. It coughed to life. As a reflex, he started to reach for the seat belt, then realized, *fuck it, I'm already dead.*

Chaz couldn't see forward; the enormous web of cracks in the windshield obscured his vision. He made a quick fist and threw it forward, punching a hole into the glass, sending tiny shards across the front hood.

His escape route — and his obstacles — now presented themselves in perfect view. Bullets continued to pound the car like a hailstorm. Possibly two or three struck his torso, but he wasn't sure and didn't have time to investigate.

Chaz threw the SUV into drive and floored it.

By the look of their surprised expressions, Chaz's attackers hadn't expected him to possess car keys. Chaz rammed the SUV directly into two soldiers and saw them slip beneath the front bumper, causing the car to rock as if jolted by speed bumps.

While most of the guards scrambled for safety and continued firing their weapons, one large man moved toward a pickup truck. Chaz realized this individual was going to pursue him on the road. He spun the steering wheel to make a sharp turn and headed right for the man and his pickup truck. The man jumped out of the way just in time as Chaz crashed hard into the side of the truck, sending it spinning across the lot into another car, wrecking them both.

With that nuisance out of the way, Chaz yanked the SUV into reverse and slammed his foot on the gas, rapidly backing away from the car lot and cracks of gunfire. He swung the vehicle into drive and aimed for a thin dirt road, not much of a road, but the only route out of this insane asylum.

By the size of the cacti and expansive desert, Chaz could tell he was still in his home state of Arizona, exact whereabouts unknown. He pushed the pedal to the floor, topped 90 miles per hour and went searching for civilization.

CHAPTER 5

Kelly, Kelly, Kelly.

Her name pounded through his head. More than anything, he sought rejuvenation in her arms. Reunited, they would go into hiding and plan their next move. They would reach out to their son, Peter, a student at Columbia University, and let him know that his father was alive, well, and kicking ass. Chaz Singleton wasn't going to lie down and die for anybody.

Chaz gunned the SUV through a long blur of barren desert. He finally reached a small paved road. It led to a bigger road that eventually joined a main highway. He discovered he was a few hours from Tucson and headed for home.

The broken windows and bullet-scarred doors prompted a lot of stares. Fortunately, the dead car owner was gone, having been dumped in the desert, where vultures and the scorching sun would accelerate disintegration. He felt bad, but the man was dead and there was nothing he could do about it. He had exchanged the dead man's clothes for his own—the blood splattered white hospital gown just didn't look good for a re-entry into society.

On the parameters of Tucson, where the traffic became heavier and the number of stares grew, he ditched the beleaguered SUV in a Taco Bell parking lot. Well versed in Tucson's public transportation system, Chaz grabbed a bus to take him across town, paying a few bucks out of the dead man's pocket. The bus let him off within walking distance of his small home in a modest community of blue and white collar working stiffs.

Chaz received plenty of stares as he climbed off the bus. He heard an old woman exclaim, "My goodness, he smelled *terrible.*"

Chaz tried to whiff his armpits but his sense of smell remained deadened. At least the stench had kept the seat next to him unoccupied.

He walked down the street, staring at the ground to avoid eye contact with any neighbors. As far as the rest of the world was concerned, he was dead. He didn't have the energy or the words to explain his resurrection right now.

The little, brick, split-level at 337 Kelton remained as cozy and charming as ever. He stepped up to the front door, tried the handle and found it locked. And he had no key.

Chaz rang the doorbell. He knocked. He rang the doorbell again. Then he circled around to the back door.

The back door was also locked, but at least it was concealed from view and no one watched as he punched a hole through a pane of glass, reached inside for the doorknob and let himself in.

"Kelly?" he called out, returning to familiar surroundings and a rush of good feelings.

"Kelly? Honey?"

Not home.

He began to worry then. He certainly couldn't stay here for very long. The madmen from the lab were not going to permit him to rejoin society and tell the tale of his blue skin and return from the dead.

Chaz walked through the living room into the kitchen and picked up a cordless phone.

He called Kelly's cell phone. He couldn't wait to hear her sweet, warm voice in his ear.

She answered on the third ring. "Hello?"

"Kelly, Kelly, it's me," he gasped. He realized his voice was still dry and hoarse, not as natural as its pre-death state.

"What?"

"Kelly, it's Chaz. I'm home."

"Chaz?"

"Please come home as soon as you can. I miss you. I have so much to tell you. We don't have much time."

"*Chaz?*"

"Yes, it's Chaz. I'm alive."

"Who is this?"

"Honey, it's Chaz."

Her voice turned cold and hard. "Fuck you, you sick bastard!"

She hung up.

Chaz called her back.

She answered immediately. "Why are you doing this?"

"I know it sounds crazy."

"How are you calling from my number?"

"It's Chaz."

"I'm going to call the police."

"No, no, honey. God, no, don't call the police."

"Stop this sick joke. I mean it!"

She hung up again.

He started to dial her a third time, then halted. What if she really did call the police?

He had some friends on the force, but they wouldn't understand, couldn't possibly understand, and one wrong phone call could bring Breck Palmer's troops to his door and endanger him, Kelly and Peter.

He decided to wait for her to return home. Hopefully it would be soon. She would see him in the flesh, get past the ludicrousness of the situation, and realize that indeed through some berserk, imperfect miracle of science, he was alive, albeit in a dead man's trappings.

"Kelly, please come home," he whispered under his breath. He peered out a window. Dusk spread shadows across the lawn. His short, glorious return to sunshine was fading back into darkness and artificial light.

Chaz walked upstairs and entered the master bathroom. He knew he should examine his appearance but it wasn't something he looked forward to.

Sure enough, he looked like death warmed over. His skin was discolored, a marble-like texture void of natural blood flow. His yellowish eyes were sunk into deep, dark wells. His teeth and gums were turning gray.

Chaz took off his shirt and dropped it to the floor. He stared at his body, once muscular, now thinned out, yet somehow even more powerful and resilient.

He could see four black holes, each about the size of a dime, located across his body: shoulder, chest, side and stomach.

They looked like enormous blackheads and itched, a bothersome intrusion. He probed one. Then he squeezed around the opening, not unlike pinching a blackhead.

He squeezed hard.

Instead of pus, he extracted a bullet. It fell to the floor and bounced off the tile.

It made him jump.

He then removed the remaining bullets from his body.

There was something about already being dead that made him harder to kill. The bullets caused little bleeding or discomfort, as if he was made of clay.

Chaz marveled over his strange invulnerability.

Why couldn't this scientific discovery be used for something good? Why was it restricted to a military cause?

Chaz washed himself with water from the sink, filling the bowl with dark crud. He felt cleaner but knew his appearance and smell would be an ongoing challenge.

Chaz entered the bedroom. A general, dull ache coated his body. While he couldn't sleep, at least he could rest. He decided to lie down on the bed until Kelly came home.

He could relax his stiff muscles…and think…and determine his next move.

As he prepared to drop onto the bed, he stopped and froze. He noticed an item of clothing on the floor that looked out of place. A pair of men's pants.

They didn't belong to Chaz.

He looked around the room and saw more curious items of clothing. A pair of dark socks beneath a chair. A crumpled shirt near the window. A pair of men's white underpants peeking out from under the bed.

Chaz felt shockwaves across his body. *Who's been sleeping in my bed?*

He grabbed the shirt and inspected it. It definitely did not belong to him. What was it doing here?

He stared at the unmade bed and imagined his wife with another man. *How could she? I've been dead less than a month!*

He paced the room, looking for more evidence. On the dresser, he found a small leather bag containing toiletries—cologne, a toothbrush, and an electric shaver.

Had this bastard moved in?

Who was he?

Chaz became obsessed. He wanted a name.

He returned downstairs to the cordless phone. He checked the log of incoming calls, clicking rapidly to go back hours, then days.

One name appeared repeatedly:

TED TUCKER.

His buddy from the construction company. Coworker, bowling partner, family friend...and now the penetrator of his wife.

"Ted, you bastard, how could you!" Chaz exclaimed, and then his thoughts turned to Kelly. "Baby, it can't be true..."

He craved more facts.

He ran to the PC in the den and logged in. He knew her password and logged into her email, frantically searching...

Ted Tucker. Ted Tucker. Ted Tucker.

He was everywhere

Chaz jabbed the keyboard, opened an email and scanned a long paragraph of filthy lust that began: "I can't wait to see you tonight and roam your curves and valleys with the tip of my tongue. Be sure to wear the hot red silk nightgown although you won't have it on for long."

Chaz jumped to another email that read, "I crave your flesh, baby." The statement made him angry...and hungry.

Another email from lover boy stirred suspicions that the romance did not just spring up in recent weeks. In the email, Ted asked Kelly, "Do you think it's been long enough that we can come out of hiding and pretend like we're beginning the relationship?"

Infuriated, Chaz switched over to the "Sent" folder to inspect emails Kelly had sent to Ted.

Some of them had torrid subject lines like "Miss you love you want you need you."

Then he found one that read: "I'm so relieved Chaz never knew about us when he was alive. Now he will never know."

Chaz roared: "You *bitch!*" into the computer monitor.

He scrolled down the long list of emails sent to Ted until he found the very first one.

April 5.

He popped it open and discovered this was the date of his funeral.

"Should I feel guilty that I feel no sadness? We watched as they lowered the coffin into the grave and I kept thinking, *I'm free, I'm free to be with my Ted.* To muster tears, I had to bring up memories of when our cat, Cuddles, got run over by the UPS truck last year. I loved that kitty."

Then Chaz read a statement that brought him to a whole new level of fury:

"It's almost too good to be true. Everything went according to plan."

What...plan?

He continued digging through the correspondence but couldn't uncover any further clues, just more expressions of love, cravings for sex and indications that this affair had been going on for at least a year.

Chaz left the trail of emails to open up a local news website, Tucson Courier. He wanted to learn more about his demise. According to Dr. Rabe, he had been electrocuted in a construction accident.

Yep, there it was.

Crane accident kills worker.

Chaz read about how the crane tipped over while transporting a heavy load of building material into the open-roofed construction of a new bank branch. As it fell, the top of the crane struck a high-voltage power line feeding the rest of the strip mall. The 9,000-volt current sent deadly electricity surging throughout the metal crane, killing its driver...Chaz Singleton. The shock killed him instantly.

The whole story did not sit comfortable with Chaz. He was well known for his meticulous attention to safety and preparation.

Why the hell did the crane tip?

Then, as he continued to read the article, transporting back to that fateful day, he recalled details that did not show up in the story, but returned to life from the far reaches of his brain.

Ted had prepared the crane that morning.

Typically, Chaz did it all himself—prepping the outrigger, a set of extended "legs" with base plates to prevent leaning, as well as the counterweights for proper balance. He had done it countless times before.

The article blamed "crane operator error" for miscalculating the counterweights and not setting up the outrigger properly. The outrigger beam snapped and the entire crane lost stability.

Ted's face appeared in Chaz's memory, backlit by the rising sun, all gentle smiles. "Hey, man, why don't you go grab coffee and a donut. I'll set up for you."

Chaz took Ted up on his offer. After all, Ted was his loyal buddy and coworker. So Chaz hopped in his car and scooted over to Klooster's, his favorite early morning stop for sugar and caffeine. He even brought back a donut for Ted.

"Thanks, dude," said Ted, biting into the donut with a mighty chomp. He made a quick gesture to the crane. "You're all set to go."

Twenty minutes later, Chaz was dead.

Everyone assumed Chaz had prepared the crane himself. Only Ted knew the truth.

And Ted knew the right way to prepare the crane...and the wrong.

Chaz returned to Kelly's emails and reread the message that had raised his suspicions.

"Everything went according to plan."

Rage engulfed Chaz. His dead tired body surged with fire, burning away the numbness.

Chaz grabbed the computer keyboard and smashed it across the monitor, creating an explosion of black plastic.

He moved across the room to a framed wedding picture, two decades old, a symbol of the vow that had now been broken. He picked it up and hurled it into the wall with a powerful slam, scattering broken glass across the floor.

Then Chaz bent forward, began to choke and tried to cry.

No tears emerged...just a single ooze of murky, dark liquid, seepage of his inner decay.

He wanted to rip apart everything in the house that represented her. He wanted to shred her clothing, demolish the furniture and destroy cherished mementos with his bare hands. He would pulverize everything in sight until his hands turned black and blue, broken and bloodied.

However, all of that would be time wasted.

He stood in the past, and the past was dead.

His new life was anywhere but here.

He knew he had to leave. Outside, darkness bled across the neighborhood. Kelly had taken the minivan, but his motorcycle remained in the garage with a full tank of gas.

He forced his attention on grabbing the necessary items for starting over in a new location, far from here.

These items boiled down to two categories: money and clothing.

He dug deep into his bottom desk drawer, behind years of accumulated miscellanea, until he retrieved a thick manila envelope, his secret stash of cash. Once upon a time, the intention of this stash was to surprise Kelly with a special gift for a special occasion—like their upcoming 25th wedding anniversary—or perhaps an extravagant vacation or the fancy sports car she coveted.

Fuck that, it's my money now, he reasoned.

He changed into fresh clothes and shoved the packet of hundred-dollar bills down the front of his pants. He grabbed a suitcase and started filling it with more clothes.

As he slammed the suitcase shut, he heard a second slam—the sound of a car door.

Chaz froze.

He heard another car door slam.

He shut off the lights. He stepped over to the window and peered outside.

Several cars had parked against the curb in front of his house. More cars were arriving.

Shit!

Chaz wished he owned a gun. He had entertained the idea for years, but burglaries were rare in his neck of the woods and it felt like a paranoid thing to do.

Now he was paranoid. He was certain these cars brought government agents who were intent on retrieving him.

How would he fight them off?

Albert Pujols.

Buried in the back of his closet, he had a baseball bat signed by the great slugger and future Hall of Famer Albert Pujols, a gift from an old friend and fellow sports nut on his 40th birthday.

The bat was worth some good money, but not more valuable than preserving his existence. Chaz grabbed the bat and headed downstairs, flipping off lights along the way.

He moved into the living room, navigating around obstacles in the dark, until he reached his big comfy chair.

He sat in the chair, keeping the bat at his side.

Chaz waited and listened.

After a long stretch of silence, he began to entertain the idea that these cars had not come for him but some social event at a neighbor's home. Maybe old Mrs. Freese was holding one of her bridge parties. Or Bobby Bowney's parents were out of town and he was bringing out the bong and Grateful Dead LPs. Or it could be Jack Oberlong gathering his buddies to watch—and wager on—surround sound sports via satellite on his 52-inch widescreen.

Chaz waited, waited and almost relaxed.

The first sound to break the silence was almost unperceivable, a slight tug at the front door, which rippled across the room with a swelling force that punched fear through his heart.

Chaz jolted up from his chair and uncoiled like a Jack in the Box. He took one step, then froze in place to continue listening. More noises joined in, scattered across different points around the house...doors, windows and possibly the roof.

He was no longer alone.

They're here.

CHAPTER 6

Intruders poured into the house.

Chaz hid in the shadows, armed with his baseball bat, getaway cash and a full tank of rage. Rage for his unfaithful wife. Rage for the betrayal of his friend. Rage for the sick and twisted government agency that brought him back from the dead to this living hell of a life...and now wanted to snuff him like a bothersome bug.

As the intruders entered, he tracked their locations in the dark, and prepared to cut a fast path through the kitchen to his garage.

I'm going to burn a hole through these bastards, hop on my chopper, and leave them behind in the desert dust.

Chaz waited. He sensed one of them creeping closer. He tightened his grip on the bat...

"I think I see something..." murmured a voice.

Chaz pounced.

He grabbed the nearest intruder by the throat, just beneath the dark outline of a head, and squeezed until the man gurgled. Chaz shoved him back to crash into a table. The rest of the intruders scrambled around the room, losing Chaz in the confusion of their own numbers as he zigzagged around them.

A gunshot lit up the room with a sudden flash. Chaz felt a slight sting in his thigh. He swung the baseball bat in a wide arc, smacking debris out of his path, including two skulls and a pair of outstretched hands.

More gunshots erupted, blasting holes in the walls and sofa cushions.

Chaz saw a thick man blocking the entry to the kitchen and plowed into him, throwing him against the garbage pail, where he fell over with the rest of the trash.

Chaz grabbed a rectangular table, the home for thousands of

family meals, and threw it into a cluster of government agents entering the kitchen. They stumbled and fell to the floor, an entanglement of arms, legs and angry shouts.

Chaz snatched the keys to his chopper off a small pegboard. He escaped into the garage, pounding the button that lifted the garage door. It groaned to life, rolling up to reveal an expanding view of freedom.

One of the government men leapt into the driveway and aimed his gun. Chaz threw his baseball bat and it bounced off the man's head, ruining his aim as he fired into the night sky.

Chaz straddled the motorcycle and kicked the engine to life with a loud, expanding roar.

More government agents spilled into the driveway. Another jumped him from behind, the first of a series to stream out of the kitchen into the garage.

Chaz grabbed his attacker and flipped him into a wall of shelves, which collapsed, raining garden tools and paint cans on the man's head.

Chaz kicked up the kickstand, leaned forward, released the clutch and plunged forward. He shot out of the garage, dodging his pursuers with sharp twists and turns, reaching out with a hard punch when they came too close.

Several men raced for their cars to continue the chase on wheels. Chaz swerved out of the driveway and into the street, directly into the path of a blue sedan driven by an innocent neighbor. The neighbor promptly spun out of control and conveniently crashed into one of the government vehicles.

Chaz accelerated down the center of the road. Several government agents tailed him, but not for long—Chaz knew this neighborhood inside out, and the chopper afforded him the ability to extend his getaway opportunities beyond common roadways.

He jumped over a curb and tore across a small playground, emptied of children for the night. The motorcycle zipped around swing sets and jungle gyms, throwing bark chips into the air. Chaz emerged from the park to enter a main road on the other side, disrupting a sleepy flow of traffic with sudden tire screeches and swerves.

As he raced faster, he could just barely feel a rush of air

against his face—an actual sensation—and it invigorated him.

He knew he couldn't ride for long out in the open for his pursuers. His first course of action was finding a good hiding place, someplace isolated and undisturbed, a sanctuary to plan his next move...

The restaurant.

One of the construction firm's future projects was tearing down Everson's, an old steak house, and replacing it with a shoe store outlet. The actual demolition was still weeks away and the restaurant sat closed, gutted and forgotten. Chaz knew the site well, having visited it with members of his crew as they reviewed the location with an architect and talked about plans for the demolition and rebuilding.

Chaz broke open the rear entrance, which was wide enough to admit his motorcycle. He pushed it inside, resealed the door and surveyed his dark, filthy surroundings.

He was in no position to complain about his accommodations. Living in a rotting carcass, the dirt and cobwebs did not faze him.

He found a thin opening between slats of a boarded up window and peered out at the street. Aside from the occasional car or truck rumbling by, he was alone.

The government agents would not find him here. He would never again return to his house or anyplace else associated with his former life.

Chaz's mind was exhausted, overstimulated after so many weeks of lying dormant.

He dropped to a dirty stretch of floorboards and tried, tried, tried to sleep. He craved the peace of unconsciousness.

Hours passed without a moment's dip into a dream state. He couldn't stop thinking about Kelly and Ted. Anger consumed him, keeping him awake.

Finally he stood up. He immediately lost his balance. A swarm of dizziness filled his head. When it cleared, he realized...

I'm starving.

He searched the restaurant but anything edible had been removed long ago. All that remained was rat droppings.

Down the road, there was a 24/7 convenience mart with slim

pickings and high prices for desperate people like himself. He decided to risk it and stick his toe back into civilization, just for a few minutes, to buy a candy bar, chips and soda.

Chaz left the motorcycle behind and walked toward the sickly glow of the food pantry. Inside, the clerk behind the counter looked even more undead than Chaz, with acne-scarred skin. Chaz dealt with him quickly, avoiding eye contact. Fortunately Chaz's disheveled appearance was the norm for this hour of the night. The only thing to raise the clerk's eyebrows was the one hundred dollar bill that had to be broken. The clerk examined it for a long moment before accepting it into the cash register.

Chaz brought the food back with him into the abandoned restaurant. He sat on a crate and began to satisfy his hunger, cramming chips and chunks of chocolate into his mouth. It tasted like nothing—just texture—but he kept eating until it was gone and washed the food down with long swigs of soda.

Minutes later, he threw it all up. His stomach rejected the food with a powerful upchuck, expelling every last trace from his body.

Chaz swore. He threw the plastic soda bottle across the room, where it bounced in the dark.

He hated his ruined body, incapable of enjoying food or any other human sensation, overcome by a dark numbness.

Chaz tried again to sleep.

Instead, he dwelled on Ted and Kelly all over again.

They were to blame.

If they hadn't killed him, he wouldn't be dead. And if he never died, he wouldn't have been kidnapped by the crazy bio-research lab conducting experiments on cadavers. Then he wouldn't be this *thing*, this walking, talking bag of bones, a pathetic and unloved zombie.

As Chaz sat alone in the dark, he could not calm himself. His anger grew. He knew he had a mission in front of him.

After all, it wasn't every day that a murder victim had the opportunity to personally avenge his death.

CHAPTER 7

As the blazing sun lifted from the mountains and splashed light across the desert valley, Chaz arrived. He parked his motorcycle down the block and around the corner from the townhouse of Ted Tucker.

He advanced on foot along the curb, a walking carcass of bubbling fury. Sure enough, the green minivan sat a few houses away, purposefully not right in front, but a sure indication that Kelly was inside the residence. She had never returned home that night.

Ted lived in a small, Mediterranean style townhouse with white stucco walls, pink tiled roofing and grill iron work. The short front yard consisted of a layer of gray gravel to cover the dirt and some cacti. His residence melded with two others of equal size and shape. From one, an old woman emerged with her poodle. She hobbled the length of her walkway to retrieve the morning paper as the dog ran circles around her. Chaz slowed his pace. The poodle noticed him, stopped, bared its teeth and began to yap.

The dog sensed something was not right with this human. He smelled different.

Chaz just stared back.

The old woman scooped up the dog, but not before shooting Chaz a stare of her own.

I know, I know, thought Chaz. *I look like hell. Just leave me alone.*

Struggling to carry both the tiny dog and her morning paper, the old woman slowly made her way back up the walk and into her home. She shut the door.

Chaz advanced to Ted's front door. He stared at it for a moment. For what he was prepared to do, knocking or buzzing the bell made an awkward introduction.

There was only one way to begin the ass kicking.

Chaz kicked down the front door.

He charged forward through the house, recognizing the layout from a few prior visits, beer and watching sports with the guys after a long day of work, one big happy family...

Chaz slammed open the door to the bedroom and two naked bodies scrambled to untangle. They peered up from a nest of sheets and pillows.

"Hello, Ted. Hello, Kelly," said Chaz.

"What the hell is this?" demanded Ted.

"I might be asking the same thing," said Chaz.

"*Chaz?*" said Kelly, squinting at him.

"It's not Chaz," said Ted. "That's crazy."

"It is Chaz, and it is crazy," he replied, stepping closer so they could get a good look.

Kelly sat up, clutching the sheets over her breasts, as if he had never seen them before. "Stay away," she said.

"Buddy, you do not have the right to break into my home," said Ted firmly.

"I can do whatever I want," said Chaz. "I don't play by the rules anymore. The rules of society, the rules of science..."

"Who are you really?" asked Kelly. "You might look like Chaz but there's something wrong with your skin...and your eyes."

"If I don't look so good, there's a simple explanation," said Chaz. "You murdered me."

The frozen look in the eyes of Ted and Kelly told him all he needed to know. The truth silenced them, at least for a moment.

"This isn't possible," said Ted. "I saw you die. I attended your funeral!"

"Yes, and it appears you brought a date," said Chaz. "You've been seeing my wife for how long...more than a year? You've been screwing her behind my back and I was too blind to see because I trusted you. I trusted both of you."

"He can't be real," said Kelly, voice swelling with panic. "It's a ghost!"

"If I was a ghost," said Chaz, "could I do this?" He reached over to the nearby dresser, which was littered with Kelly's belongings—her purse, makeup, hairspray, bra—and swept it all to the floor with one big swat of his arm.

Ted jumped out of the bed and began pulling on his jeans. "You are going to leave."

"No," said Chaz calmly. "I'm afraid not. You can't get rid of me, no matter how hard you try."

Barefoot and shirtless, Ted advanced on Chaz. He examined him, hands balled into fists. "I'm not going to tell you again..."

"The news reports said 'crane operator error,'" said Chaz. "You set up that crane. You did the outrigging and counterbalances. You made sure the crane would tip. You knew it would fall right into that power line and kill me instantly."

Ted stood toe-to-toe with Chaz. "You can't prove a thing. That crane was your responsibility."

"I don't have to prove anything. I take care of my own justice now."

Ted reeled. "Shit, man. Your breath really stinks."

"Sucks being dead."

"Yeah, well if you don't leave my house, I'll gladly kill you again."

"And how do you propose to do that?"

Ted turned away from Chaz and looked to Kelly, who remained sitting up in the bed, watching with wide eyes and a tight grip on the sheets. "Honey," he said, "I recommend you look away. You're not going to want to see this."

Ted stepped to the dresser. He opened the top drawer, reached deep and brought out a small, snub-nosed revolver. He pointed it at Chaz.

"I am merely protecting myself and my loved one from a home invasion by a blue-skinned psycho, claiming to be Chaz Singleton. I don't care who or what you are, you do not break into my home, my bedroom and threaten me. Good riddance, trash. You are history."

Chaz stood there, bored and unmoved, as Ted fired the gun into his chest.

The sudden noise caused Kelly to scream.

Chaz remained standing, a red, drippy hole in his chest.

"Are you done now?" he asked Ted plainly.

"Holy shit," said Ted.

Chaz moved forward, grabbed the arm that held the gun and yanked hard. He threw Ted into the wall with a mighty thud that knocked framed pictures to the floor.

Kelly screamed again. Ted came charging off the floor to fight back and the two men locked into a fierce exchange of blows. Although Ted was a larger man, Chaz did not feel the impact of his punches. Kelly joined the fray, jumping on Chaz's back, and he flipped her against the bed where she bounced off the mattress and landed on the floor. She cried out in pain.

Ted exploded all over Chaz, throwing a flurry of punches. Chaz fought back with an animal ferocity that overtook him like a demonic possession. Everything became a fast motion blur against a spinning background

— and then Ted squealed.

The frenzy slammed to a halt. The room grew still and quiet. Ted stood doubled over. Chaz watched as Ted slowly began to straighten up, clutching his left arm with the bloodied fingers of his right hand.

"Son of a bitch..." sputtered Ted. "You *bit* me."

Chaz stood in shock at the revelation. He didn't remember doing it, but as his tongue slid across the inside of his mouth, he felt wetness...and a chunk of something grisly and gristly.

A fantastic sensation filled his head and then swarmed his entire body. It reminded him of the feedings at the lab, which became highly anticipated events of rare physical stimulation.

"He *bit* you!" exclaimed Kelly, still on the floor, seated on her naked butt.

"Hurts like hell!" exclaimed Ted.

Chaz realized the raw insanity of his actions.

Then he continued to chew...and swallowed. His throat constricted with a hearty gulp.

Ted lifted his fingers off the wound, finding an excavation caused by the jagged arc of deep, individual teeth marks. He shouted "What the fuck!"

Chaz shuddered with gratification as the nourishment slid into his belly.

Kelly rose to her feet and ran over to Ted to examine the wound. "Oh my God!" she shrieked.

Chaz turned and caught a glimpse of himself in a mirror above the dresser. Bright red lips sent trickles of blood down his chin, the only vibrant color on an otherwise grayish blue face. He looked like a monster, more real and harrowing than a thousand horror movies.

Kelly grabbed a piece of clothing from the floor, wadded it tight and pressed it against Ted's wound. She cradled him as he whimpered over his missing flesh. His blood created red splotches on her naked body. She stared hard at Chaz, who remained standing in the center of the room.

"What *are* you?" she hissed at him.

Chaz burped.

After a moment, he broke out of his daze. He quickly left the bedroom, using his sleeve to wipe the food off his face. He departed from the townhouse and returned to his motorcycle, kicking it to life and roaring into the rising sun.

CHAPTER 8

7:45 a.m.

In the bathroom, Kelly cleaned Ted's wound, bandaged it tight and stopped the bleeding. The blood loss made him woozy, but he remained focused and firm on one absolute:

"I am not going to the hospital," he said.

"But honey, it's a really bad bite. You need stitches. It could be infected. You saw how filthy he looked, God only knows what—"

"I said, *no hospital*," said Ted, shaking off the pain, examining the bandage. Some blood still seeped through.

"But—"

He grabbed her shoulder with his good arm. "Think this through, Kelly. What are we going to tell them? So he bit me. What we did to him was a lot worse. It's a bad path to go down."

"But how do we know it was really him?"

"I don't know. I don't get any of this. If it's somebody pretending to be him... Why? If it really is him...how?"

"Maybe the electrocution didn't kill him," said Kelly. "He survived and faked his own death in order to catch us."

"How do you fake your own death?"

"I don't know! There are people you can pay off, I'm sure of it."

"That's absurd."

"More absurd than his ghost showing up and attacking us?"

Ted just shrugged. He looked at himself in the small mirror over the sink. He looked pale.

"I don't feel so good..."

10:23 a.m.

"Can we go to the hospital now?"

Ted shook his head at her. He lay in bed with the sheets and blankets pulled high. "No."

"You're sick. You've lost a lot of blood..."

"I just have a small fever. I'm okay, I'm..." Then his sentences trailed into mumbles.

He shut his eyes. "Bright in here."

Kelly paced around him. "I don't like this."

"I just wanna sleep, hon. The bastard woke us up, I'm tired."

"I'm scared."

"We'll be okay..." He rolled to one side, then the other, trying to find a comfortable position. "I just want to rest."

1:09 p.m.

She watched him sleep.

He continued to perspire, so she placed a wet washrag on his forehead. He stirred and muttered, "Thanks."

"If you don't get better, I'm calling the doctor."

"I'm fine."

"I'm serious."

"Shut up." He moved the wet washrag from his forehead to cover his eyes.

2:11 p.m.

"What? What?"

"You've been thrashing in your sleep."

"Leave me alone."

"But Ted..."

"Leave me alone, bitch."

"Fine!" She stormed out of the bedroom and left for the den to watch TV.

3:31 p.m.

After watching a lurid daytime talk show with chair throwing, she returned to the bedroom to check on Ted.

He was tucked under the sheets, a big lump, very still.

She leaned over and gently peeled back the covers to expose the back of his head. She reached out and stroked his hair.

His hand shot out and grabbed her arm. She squeaked and pulled away. He murmured, "Mmmmmm." She took it as a gesture he wanted her to join him in the bed.

He must be getting better, she thought to herself. He's horny.

She disrobed and climbed under the sheets next to him. He turned toward her and buried his face in her breasts.

His face was cold. His tongue was even colder.

"Honey, you're freezing," she said. "Are you sure you don't want a doctor?"

He replied, "Mmmmmmrrrrgghh."

She giggled because his licking and kisses tickled. Then he nibbled.

"Mmmmmm," he said again.

"Mmmmmm," she replied, turned on. She felt him transform into a familiar, slobbering mass of arousal.

His head lowered and she felt his mouth teasing, sucking, nipping.

"Ow, don't, you'll leave a hickey," she giggled.

He continued to journey his lips down her body.

She moaned and shuddered. "Eat me," she ordered him.

Kelly's screams turned from ecstasy to terror as he proceeded to do just that.

CHAPTER 9

Chaz sat on a crate inside the abandoned restaurant, weighed down by the horror of his behavior at Ted's townhouse.

I'm a cannibal.

In a flash of raw instinct, he bit a man...tore off a piece of his arm...and digested it.

"I can't live like this," Chaz said out loud in the surrounding dark and dust.

The townhouse confrontation kept replaying in his head. A fistfight, the adrenalin pumping, and then a loss of control as he lunged teeth first at his victim.

On one level, he was terrified and disgusted by his behavior.

On another level, recalling it stirred more unnatural urges.

Earlier, he had discovered some of Ted's blood on his shirt. His first reaction had been to bring it to his mouth, like a little child licking the last few drops of ice cream from the bottom of the bowl.

Chaz rose from the crate and paced the empty, gutted restaurant. He walked to the front of the building, where a ray of light emerged from between slats of a boarded up window. Bending down and positioning himself just right, he could see the sidewalk. Pedestrians strolled in and out of view.

He watched a young woman walk by. She wore a sleeveless tank top with her arms and flat belly exposed.

He craved her soft skin.

More pedestrians stepped into his sight and every one of them riled his urges. The more flesh exposed, the more his jaws began to gnash involuntarily. He experienced an unusual wetness in his mouth.

I'm salivating.

Guilt and shame washed over him, but he could not move away from the peephole. He couldn't budge his thoughts. They kept returning to the same default: tasty humans.

The chunk of arm had just been a snack, an appetizer, and he craved a main course. When a beautiful redhead came into view in skimpy shorts, displaying juicy thighs, he lost his mind. He scampered out of the restaurant and circled to the front sidewalk, his brain pumping out possible lines to lure her into the abandoned building.

"Hi," he said.

"Hi," she said, wrinkling her nose. She gave him a funny look, no doubt because he looked funny, not ha ha funny, but creepy funny, a cartoon with tattered clothing, sunken eyes and bluish-gray skin.

He let her go without another word.

Some common sense kicked back in.

Are you crazy? he asked himself. *What were you thinking?*

He hated the urges. He wanted to remove that part of his brain.

More people headed his way on the sidewalk, including an elderly man with a cane and a pudgy child. The possibility that he might lose control and gnaw on their limbs delivered fear deep in his soul. Every living person was a potential meal.

As he turned to head back inside the restaurant, his eyes caught a Tucson Courier headline pressed against the window of a newspaper box.

He dug coins out of his pocket, paid for a paper and brought it with him into the abandoned building.

He read the article: *Fire consumes government research lab.*

The article confirmed his fears: A massive cover-up buried the truth.

The referenced "research lab" was the underground bunker where Dr. Rabe and his cohorts had been toying with the doomed zombie experiment. However, for the media and general public, the purpose of the lab became far more generic: "defense research."

An unfortunate "accident" caused by a "chemical reaction" in one of the "weapon labs" caused the explosion, which incinerated the entire facility and killed everyone inside.

"These men died doing important and noble work for their

country," said Breck Palmer, Director of Research Studies. "While this accident is a terrible tragedy, it will not curtail our ongoing commitment to ensure the safety and security of every American through a fully prepared and state-of-the-art military defense. We are conducting an internal investigation to make sure an accident like this never happens again. I ask the community to pray for the loss of this dedicated and talented staff, some of the best and brightest scientists in the country."

Chaz felt more frightened and alone than ever.

The dead scientists, the destroyed zombies...all incinerated in a powerful blast. No evidence. No witnesses. No truth. Only a warm blanket of lies.

Under the strictest of orders and threats, the participants in the zombie experiment had kept the secrets of their research from their loved ones, who remained oblivious. The newspaper quoted Margaret Delphy, the widow of one of the killed scientists: "This is a terrible shock. But it's also a reality of the job. We were well aware of the risks of advanced weapons research. I am proud of my husband's dedication to his country and I know that he made a difference in moving our defense program forward."

Chaz dropped the newspaper to the floor. Margaret Delphy's husband had died at the hands of his employer, probably from a bullet to his back as he tried to flee for his life.

Everyone involved with the project had perished to ensure the secrets never leaked.

Only one survivor surfaced from the project team and his smarmy lies were splashed all over the media coverage, efficiently snuffing any potential flames of controversy.

Breck Palmer.

CHAPTER 10

Sipping a tall, Styrofoam cup of coffee, Breck Palmer read the Tucson Courier's coverage of the military lab accident on his iPad. He sat behind the wheel of his black sedan, parked against the curb on a quiet suburban street under blue skies.

He read the article three times, nodding along the way, finding no worrisome bumps as his eyes traveled the columns of copy. The reporter got it right. All was good. Palmer would not have to pursue drastic measures to address unauthorized extracurricular research. Two years ago, there had been a nosy reporter obsessed with learning more about secret military operations that the general public did not need to know.

Gerald Schmidt. Poor Gerald was promptly killed by a hit-and-run driver during an early morning jog. The tires rolled right over his head, a terrible, terrible tragedy. The driver of the vehicle was never found.

Fortunately for the reporter on today's story, he got it correct, including every word of Palmer's quotes.

As long as a follow-up story did not appear, the lab explosion would quickly fade from public memory, replaced by the latest celebrity scandals and sports scores. Given the ongoing "spot checks" of the past year, Palmer felt confident the lab staff had not shared the realities of their work with their spouses or anyone else, staying true to their nondisclosure agreements and the threat of a lifetime in prison for treason.

Palmer shut down the iPad. He looked out his windshield at the quiet suburban home across the street, the residence of Chaz Singleton.

Only one loose end remained and it was a big, lumbering one. The damned, escaped "smart zombie" created by Dr. Rabe. Chaz knew enough to be dangerous and posed a threat to mankind. A single carrier of the flesh-eating virus was one too many.

The possibility of Chaz returning home at this point was slim to none. More surprisingly, his wife had yet to surface, and she could be a valuable conduit back to her husband.

The house displayed a few remnants of the raid the night before, including a broken window and damaged front door. So far, none of the neighbors had grown too curious and contacted the cops, a fact verified by secret taps monitoring the local police dispatch center.

Palmer could count on one hand the number of people remaining who knew the truth about Operation Invincible. All of them could be trusted, which was why they lived. Two of them were currently dedicated to a round-the-clock manhunt to uncover Chaz's whereabouts.

As Palmer continued his surveillance on the Singleton house, one of his men called to deliver a snippet of recent discovery.

"His wife has been involved with another man," came the report. "His name is Ted Tucker. They had been keeping their relationship a secret until recently. He used to work with the subject. I have his address. Do you want me to go check it out?"

"No," said Palmer. "I'll handle it. Give me the location."

Palmer entered the address into his GPS. Then he asked, "What about the subject?"

"We're still looking," came the reply. "No clues yet, but we believe he's still in the general area, hiding out."

"We'll find him," said Palmer. "Sooner or later, he'll make himself known. He'll get hungry..."

**

As dusk lowered darkness across the panoramic desert, Palmer pulled up in front of the townhouse of Ted Tucker. A green minivan sat down the block. A quick check with his source verified the owner to be Kelly Singleton.

He opened a small case on the seat next to him and extracted a .38 handgun. If cooperation didn't come naturally, it would be enforced.

Palmer looked around, observed no witnesses and climbed out of his car. He headed up the walkway for the front door.

He was prepared to break it down, but didn't need to. He turned the handle and the door opened.

Palmer entered, gun drawn.

He gently closed the door behind him.

He stood silent on the carpet and listened.

He heard strange noises coming from another room of the house. It sounded wet and sloppy, like a dog wolfing down a soggy bowl of pet food. As Palmer advanced, he could hear small, guttural moans blended with the smacking noises.

Palmer kept the gun raised. He rounded a corner and faced the kitchen. Two sets of eyes looked up at him. Ted Tucker and Kelly Singleton sat on the floor, mouths filled with bloody, dripping hunks of human flesh, leaned over a sprawled, dead teenage boy in sneakers, blue jeans and a t-shirt. A spilled pizza box lay on the floor next to him, the pizza still whole and untouched. The boy, however, remained neither whole nor untouched. Both ears had been gnawed off, along with considerable portions of his throat and arms. The kitchen floor was lost under a long pool of blood.

Kelly sat nude and unashamed with raw, open bite marks down the front of her body.

Palmer aimed the gun at her, then at Ted, then back to Kelly. They didn't appear flustered by his presence, returning their deadened gaze to their feeding. Palmer sensed that if he stepped any closer, they would growl at him like a dog protecting a bone.

"You poor, sick savages," muttered Palmer. The gory scene before him told him everything he needed to know:

Chaz had been here.

Chaz had bit them both, or maybe one of them who turned on the other.

In any case, they now fed on a third party whose presence was increasingly clear.

The two zombies had gotten the munchies and called for a pizza delivery boy. Now they feasted.

Palmer aimed for the center of Ted Tucker's forehead. Right before he pulled the trigger, Ted looked at him, drooling long strands of blood from his lips. The impact of the bullet sent Ted reeling back against the kitchen cabinets, where he went limp and still.

Her feeding rudely interrupted, Kelly jumped to her bare feet. The naked, partially chewed zombie woman lunged at Palmer, her mouth still stuffed with pink pizza boy flesh. Palmer fought her off, keeping a safe distance from her gnashing, red teeth. As she thrashed, he aimed the gun and fired—missing his target, striking her heart instead. She came at him again. He fired once more, this time popping a red hole between her eyes. After a spasmodic dance, she dropped to the floor.

Two down, one to go.

The pizza boy would soon succumb to the virus and begin his own feeding frenzy. Palmer made sure that would not happen with a bullet to the dead boy's brain. Blood splashed across the unwanted pepperoni pizza, soaking into the tomato paste.

"What a mess," mumbled Palmer.

Tucking the gun into his waistband, under his shirt, he moved quickly through the house and out the front door.

He hurried across the gravel front yard and into his black sedan. He started up the car, roaring the engine to life in the still night. He had one more duty to take care of—destroying all evidence of this bizarre cannibal feast.

Palmer left the site and returned 20 minutes later with two cans of gasoline. He consumed the house in a blazing inferno.

CHAPTER 11

Chaz struggled through a sleepless night. He wondered if he would ever sleep again, if rampant insomnia was yet another curse of the undead. Harsh images and frantic thoughts raced through his mind, many of them flashes from long-forgotten moments of his life, as if his brain was full and he could only scroll through previously recorded data. Crazy bits of his childhood merged with melancholy clips from his marriage, interacting with resurfaced anger at an old boss, then slipping into mundane tasks, like polishing the chrome on his motorcycle, over and over.

"Go away," he mumbled in the dark to the disobedient brain that ran in hyperactive circles, locked in an attic of memories.

Early morning sunlight leaked into the room, sending him a message to get up and concede defeat in the battle for sleep. He cursed the forced consciousness. He craved a dark, forgetful place where he could escape and let go. The more he thought about it, the more he realized that it wasn't slumber he craved, but a true and final demise—The Big Sleep.

Whatever one called this current existence, it wasn't living. Ridiculous, horrible, shameful and painful, yes. Living? Not so much.

Then Chaz brightened with a single thought. *Hey, I'll kill myself.*

He had seen a long portion of rubber tubing in an area of the restaurant that once housed the kitchen. He found the tubing, liked its length and strength, and began searching for a place to hang out. On the other side of the room, he found a thick pipe running along the ceiling. Grabbing a chair, he tied the rubber tubing to the pipe with a firm knot and fashioned a noose at the other end.

He placed the noose around his neck and tightened it for a snug fit.

No more hiding. No more eating people. No more reflecting

on an existence cut short by betrayal and revived by mad scientists. No more crushing despair...

Chaz kicked the chair away and it toppled to one side, out of the reach of his dangling legs.

The pipe groaned from his weight, the rubber tubing stretched, but everything held and his feet did not touch the ground.

Chaz shut his eyes and felt the squeeze around his throat shut off the flow of oxygen like a valve.

Pleased, he hung in silence, immobile.

Forty-five minutes later, he was pissed. This was not working. He did not feel his existence leaking away, his soul departing for the heavens or even that other place. He was just a dangling slab of meat, idle and bored.

Chaz gave it another 15 minutes, but his condition did not change. Those rejuvenation scientists had done their work *too* well. Damn it, Dr. Rabe!

He reached up, gripped the tubing and pulled hard. After a few minutes of tugging and twisting with all of his zombie might, the noose tore apart and he landed on the floor.

He stomped around his surroundings, trying to find something, anything that would lend a hand to his goal.

Most of the restaurant's contents had been cleared out, but he did find a few items left by the construction crew: a couple of hard hats, a pair of thick gloves, a lunch box, a scattering of screws and fasteners, and a small pile of tools.

Hammer... Screwdriver... Wrench... Box cutter...

Stop—hold on that. His eyes skipped back to the last item. A box cutter with a nice pointy blade.

Chaz grabbed it, tucked himself in a corner and proceeded to cut his wrists.

He made a mess but could not inflict serious harm. Some lazy, old blood leaked out, then clotted. The skin turned more weird colors and puffed up. He stabbed and sliced, but the expected red flow was never more than a brownish trickle. The Grim Reaper was not interested.

Chaz threw the tool across the room, stomped around in more circles, then had to take his energy outside.

In the bright light, thrust into clear reality, his predicament felt even more absurd. He headed down the sidewalk, receiving occasional but well-deserved stares. He knew he looked weird and his scowl would not come off.

He walked swiftly, without tiring, for ten blocks, entering the edge of downtown Tucson. He blended in with the bigger crowd, where many of the living already looked like zombies, blank faced and shuffling off to work, caught up in their own private version of hell.

He stopped at the foot of the Glaza Building, a 16-story office building he had worked on two years ago. His crew helped renovate the landmark building with new elevators, the installation of fire sprinklers, a new lobby, and an upgrade of the heating, ventilation and air conditioning systems.

Chaz knew his way around the building, including where to find a service entry for skipping past security and the right combination of elevators, stairways and ladders that would lead him to the rooftop.

A drop from sixteen floors should kill most anything, he told himself.

Within minutes, he was stepping to the edge of the roof. On this blue and sunny day, he was struck for a moment by the glorious view of his surroundings—downtown Tucson and its panoramic desert colors with majestic mountains in the distance reaching for the sky.

This is gorgeous, this is perfect, he told himself. *Take it all in and exhale everything else. Make this your final image. We come, we go, but the beauty of God's earth outlasts us all.*

Chaz closed the book on his existence, said a simple "the end," and dropped from the ledge into a rush of air.

He felt no fear, just a strange fascination, watching the concrete alley below rush up to meet him as his ears filled with the roar of his descent.

POW.

Blackness. Good.

No pain. Good.

Then Chaz realized he shouldn't be aware of anything at all—not darkness or lack of pain. Not good.

Chaz opened his eyes. He did not see angels or demons. He saw an ordinary fat woman with a thick neck and dangling pearls leaned over him with a face dominated by bright lipstick and harsh eye shadow.

"Oh my Gawwwd," she gasped.

Behind the woman he saw blue sky and a twirling pair of birds. He tilted his head and caught a glimpse of the Glaza Building ascending sixteen stories from where he lay.

"Shit," he said.

"Don't move!" said the fat woman. An older man in a hat and thick glasses also came into view, joined by a tense young couple holding hands, bug-eyed. They began chattering among themselves.

"Did you see that?"

"He fell off the roof."

"He jumped!"

"Look, he's moving."

"How can he be alive?"

"Call 911."

"No!" shouted Chaz forcefully, joining the conversation. "Don't call 911!"

He started to sit up and in unison they all yelled at him: "Stay still!" "You're hurt!" "Don't move!" "We'll get you help!"

"I don't want help."

"You're in shock—"

"Just a scratch. I'll be okay."

"Don't be crazy."

"I'm fine," said Chaz, and he stood up. The bystanders delivered a collective gasp. More onlookers rushed to the scene, thickening the circle around him.

When he tried to slip through them, they moved to block his path. One even laid a hand on him, which he promptly removed.

"Don't touch me!"

"We're calling an ambulance."

"Please don't do that." But it was too late. He saw at least half a dozen people on cell phones.

"I don't believe this!" said a skinny, bearded man who had arrived on his bike. He aimed his cell phone to take a snapshot. "I gotta get a picture of this guy."

Chaz swatted the cell phone out of his hand, sending it scattering across the alley.

"Asshole!" yelled the cyclist.

Chaz pushed his way through the crowd and made a run for it. At first, they were too stunned to pursue him. But then several broke out in a trot to follow. One continued to insist, "But mister, you're hurt!"

Chaz didn't want to argue, but he felt just fine, thank you. His body ached like one big bruise, but that was about it.

Chaz turned out of the alley and plunged into thick pedestrian traffic. He snaked through openings in the throngs of people. When he felt he had eluded his pursuers, he slipped around a corner and entered a diner he knew, Rizzo's Grill. The diner had a funky L-shaped layout and more than anything, he coveted one of the booths in the back, out of view from the windows and most of the other customers.

He was relieved to see an empty booth at the very back, unpopular due to its proximity to the kitchen and restrooms. He slid into it, sunk his head in a menu and prayed that no one had followed him in.

After ten minutes, he felt good that the well-meaning mob had lost his trail. He would become an urban legend, the man who fell from the sky, the suicide jumper who survived without a scratch, a subject of stories no one would ever believe, except perhaps a supermarket tabloid, alongside Big Foot and UFOs, and he would be happy to leave it at that.

A waitress showed up and to maintain his occupancy of the booth he ordered an omelet breakfast he probably wouldn't and couldn't eat.

After she left, he sat back and roamed his hands across his legs, arms and ribcage, looking for any signs of serious damage and finding none. Defiantly, his body remained in one piece, no more scuffled than the shoes on his feet.

Chaz pondered his next move, but the thoughts were cut short by an interruption from a familiar voice.

"Holy shit, Chaz, is that you?"

CHAPTER 12

Greg Jensen slid into the booth, sitting directly across from Chaz. His jovial face lit up with awe. "Chaz... Chaz Singleton, right? I don't believe it!"

Greg lived two blocks from Chaz. They had met years ago at the Waverly Golf Club and subsequently become golfing buddies. Greg worked in marketing for the local minor league baseball team and occasionally scored Chaz free tickets. A few times each year, they went out to eat with their wives, exploring new restaurants in downtown Tucson.

"Oh my God," said Jensen. "What gives? I went to your funeral!"

Chaz smiled, nodded and kept his cool. "Chaz...yes... He's my twin brother. I'm Chip. He got the good looks, I got the bad skin."

"I'm so sorry. I didn't know Chaz had a twin."

"Well, yes. He doesn't mention me much. We don't get along...*didn't* get along."

"You weren't at the funeral."

Chaz shrugged. "I was traveling for business. International. Beijing. Couldn't make it. I know that sounds cold, but we really didn't get along. He hated my guts. Better for his family that I didn't go."

"Incredible," said Jensen, still taking it in. "All this time, he never mentioned you."

Chaz couldn't help asking, "How was...the funeral?"

"Beautiful, man," said Jensen. "You should have been there."

"Nice turnout?"

"Huge turnout. People loved Chaz. His wife was a wreck. One of Chaz's construction buddies had to hold her up the whole time."

"Ted Tucker," muttered Chaz, resisting the urge to replace the second T with an F.

"Excuse me?" said Jensen.

"Nothing. Go on."

Jensen sat back. "The highlight of the whole thing by far was Chaz's son, Peter."

Chaz straightened up. "Peter?"

"I always thought he was kind of aloof, you know how kids get. But he delivered the most heartbreaking eulogy I have ever heard. There wasn't a dry eye in the house."

"Really?" said Chaz, feeling a sudden sensation stirring in his heart—an awakening of feelings emerging from deep in his numb zombie physiology.

"Yeah, they have the speech posted on the funeral home's website," said Jensen. "It'll choke you up. Obviously this kid was rocked hard. And he delivered it so beautiful, like poetry. You could tell he was expressing things he had never expressed before. He said he never told his dad, 'I love you' while he was alive, and now he regretted it, and he would never get another chance."

Chaz fell silent.

The waitress delivered a cheese omelet. Chaz just stared at it. He knew if he tried to eat it, he would gag.

"You want this?" said Chaz to Jensen, shoving the plate at him. "I'm really not that hungry."

"Serious?"

Chaz stood up and dropped some bills on the table to cover the check. "I have to go. But it was really nice seeing you again—I mean, meeting you. I appreciate hearing about the funeral. I'm sorry I missed it. I really am."

Jensen stared up and pointed at him. "What happened to your neck?"

Chaz realized the noose must have left a pretty bad rope burn.

"Rash," said Chaz. "Enjoy the omelet." He quickly left the diner.

CHAPTER 13

Chaz moved quickly through the downtown pedestrian traffic, avoiding eye contact with everyone, advancing several blocks until he reached his destination: the Tucson Public Library.

He waited for a turn, then took a seat at one of the public computers and dived into the Internet. His shambled condition did not look out of place among the other derelicts and homeless patrons who coveted free web access.

Chaz looked up his obituary. He found the funeral home web site. He began reading through the many tributes posted by friends and family. Each one delivered a warm glow to his heart, surfacing a depth of feeling he hadn't experienced since before his death. He nearly felt human again.

Then he found his son's tribute.

Peter flew in from the east coast, mid semester, to cope with the sudden shock of his father's untimely death. A wonderful, confident, happy young man had been reduced to a broken down child, lost in sadness.

Chaz read his son's tribute and cried. Black tears plunked down on the keyboard. He had to wipe his eyes and look away from the screen.

As he collected himself, he caught the stare of an older, grizzled man at a nearby PC. From an unshaven face heavy with wrinkles, the man's sharp blue eyes pierced Chaz with a look of surprise and apprehension. Chaz stared back and watched the man shift his gaze to his computer monitor, then back at Chaz, then back to the computer monitor, and then again to Chaz.

The old man stood up, mouth agape, and staggered away from the table.

Chaz watched him go, then stood up himself. He circled around to the PC where the old man had sat. He looked at the screen.

Chaz faced a sketchy, black and white reflection of himself, a loose charcoal drawing accompanied by a news headline: *Suspect tied to deadly home blaze.*

"Oh no," said Chaz softly. He dropped into the chair to continue reading.

"Tucson police are working with officials to identify three badly burned bodies at the scene of a deadly townhouse fire at the residence of Theodore Tucker, a 39-year-old construction worker. Tucker is believed to be among the victims, in addition to Jerzy Pucinski, a delivery employee from Papa Dini's Pizza. Pucinski's car was discovered by police parked in Tucker's driveway at 862 Alemeda Road. A night manager at the restaurant confirmed a pizza delivery at the residence from which Pucinski did not return. The third victim has not been identified."

Chaz continued reading, stunned. The story reported that a neighbor had seen a suspicious white male enter the townhouse earlier in the day. Chaz remembered the old woman with the poodle. She had provided police with a detailed description, resulting in the black and white sketch.

"Police are actively searching for the unidentified visitor for questioning. Anyone with information is urged to contact the Tucson Police."

Chaz leaped from the chair and hurried out of the computer room.

As he entered the main library corridor, he saw the grizzled old man talking excitedly with a nervous male librarian who nodded while reaching for his cell phone. As Chaz scooted past them, the old man stabbed a finger in his direction and exclaimed, "That's HIM!"

"Sir!" shouted the librarian.

The library patrons turned to look at Chaz as he ran for the exit. A woman with an armload of books didn't get out of the way fast enough and he plowed into her, sending the books scattering in all directions.

Chaz escaped outdoors and dashed back into the sidewalk crowd. He did not look back. He buried himself in the pedestrian traffic.

He knew his time in Tucson was over. He had to leave the

city as quickly as possible.

Chaz ran back to the abandoned restaurant to get his motorcycle. He circled to the rear of the shuttered building and slipped in through the back door.

Entering the sudden blackness of the barren restaurant, his eyes lost their focus. He stepped forward, arms outstretched.

A voice greeted him from somewhere deep in the shadows.

"Hello, Chaz. I've been waiting for you."

CHAPTER 14

Breck Palmer stepped forward, gun drawn.

Chaz froze. He looked over at his motorcycle, a good 30 feet away. Palmer said, "I'm afraid you can forget it. You're not going anywhere."

"What do you want with me?"

"I am your assassin. You are the last zombie. Until you are destroyed, a threat exists to all of mankind."

"I'm honored."

Palmer advanced until he stood a few feet from Chaz. He continued to point the handgun at him. "A sense of humor. I like that in a zombie."

"I'm not like the others."

"I know. You are that rare breed, a 'smart zombie.' An interesting mutation, to be sure, but in the end, just as dangerous. You are aware of what you need to do to survive?"

"Yes."

"And that anyone you bite becomes infected?"

Chaz nodded.

"Clearly that won't do," said Palmer. "You're a rational man, you get it. So let's get this over with and return you where you belong. Think of the novelty. You get to experience death...twice."

"But I'm already dead," said Chaz. "How do you kill something that no longer lives?"

"Your rotting bag of bones still has a command center. It's called a brain. Kill the brain and you kill the zombie. That's how we dispatched the zombies at the lab before we incinerated them. That's how I took care of your construction worker friend, the pizza boy and your lovely naked wife... before I burned the house down."

Chaz's mind flashed to the news story about the townhouse blaze, a convenient way to obscure three zombies shot dead.

Palmer said, "I have one important question before I put you down for good. Listen carefully. Who else have you chewed on? I need to know. We can't have others like you."

"Nobody," said Chaz.

"Bullshit," responded Palmer. "Don't pretend like you can control the urges..."

"I've tried."

"You might as well tell me now. None of your victims will stay secret. I will find out, and I will destroy them."

"There are no more," said Chaz.

Palmer sighed. "Very well." He steadied the gun, making careful aim for the center of Chaz's forehead.

Chaz thought about dying for good. A short while ago, he longed for it. But something in him stirred, a sudden craving...for life.

He jumped just in time as the gun fired, the bullet whizzing past his ear. Chaz ran deeper into the abandoned restaurant, remembering the location of the construction crew's gear. More shots rang out and a bullet punctured his back, a sharp irritation like a bee sting.

Chaz reached his destination, swooped down his arm and picked up a yellow hardhat. He placed it on his head.

Palmer came at him, firing the gun.

Two bullets meant for Chaz's brain pinged off the helmet.

Palmer's expression turned from surprise to horror as he realized this enabled Chaz to turn the attack on him.

Chaz charged Palmer. Palmer tried one last time, unsuccessfully, to penetrate the helmet with gunfire.

Then Chaz was upon him.

Chaz felt himself lose all control. His jaws began to clatter. He bit into the sleeve of Palmer's shirt and tore away fabric, but failed to reach flesh.

Palmer punched Chaz in the face and Chaz hit back, sending Palmer crashing hard into a wall, triggering a large puff of dust. When Palmer sprang back to his feet, he threw a fistful of debris at Chaz, including nails and screws. Chaz felt them strike his eyes and face, but it didn't stop him from grabbing Palmer and tossing him across the room with a loud, animal-like roar.

It felt good.

Palmer came back at Chaz with a large board and cracked it across Chaz's midsection, breaking the board into two pieces. The sudden shock of pain faded fast and then Palmer was on his ass again in another part of the room.

Chaz dashed for his motorcycle. He jumped aboard and kicked it to life. The engine boomed with a powerful echo that shook the walls.

Palmer rose to his feet and ran to block Chaz's escape.

Bad move. The motorcycle's immediate acceleration thrust it forward with such force that Palmer became a minor obstacle, thrown out of the way as he fired one last desperate bullet into the ceiling.

Chaz powered the bike forward, braced himself and crashed through the brittle back door, splintering it into wood pieces, emerging into the bright daylight.

He spun the bike away from the abandoned restaurant, kicking up gravel and dirt as he entered an alley. He roared toward the main road.

Chaz aimed the motorcycle between two sluggish lanes of traffic to create his own path. He raced through downtown Tucson and shot onto the expressway ramp.

Chaz watched the speedometer climb...70...80...90.

The yellow hardhat flew off his head and disappeared.

He experienced a burst of exhilaration. He felt better somehow, cleansed, because he had a mission. Everything became crystal clear with a singular focus.

Chaz wanted to see his son, Peter. He had unfinished business. He wanted his son to know that he existed, he loved, and he cared. He wanted to communicate with his son in ways that had eluded their relationship for so many years.

They never had the chance to express themselves when Chaz was alive. Now God, or perhaps the Devil, had given him a second chance.

CHAPTER 15

Chaz cut across Arizona on his Harley, speeding like a gunshot through long stretches of desert, liberated by the fact that he could outrun the highway patrol and survive most any accident.

He let the needle dip into the 90s and beyond. The speed provided excellent progress to his getaway and delivered a high-octane thrill he could not have indulged in during his living years.

He crossed through the San Simon Valley and into New Mexico, welcomed by stark ghost towns lost in time to a bygone era. He was just another restless spirit blown in by the wind. When he reached Las Cruces, he headed northeast, entering the treacherous terrain of the Sacramento Mountains. Rising sharply out of the desert, the tree-lined elevations comprised the southern end of the Rocky Mountains, thick with vegetation and cut deep with canyons.

He maneuvered the steep ridges, calculating the concise angle of every sharp turn, keeping an eye on the long drop to the tiny pines far below. The difficult terrain ensured his privacy. He had taken a detour off the major highway, determined to lose anyone hoping to track his path.

Chaz knew Breck Palmer would continue pursuing him, and he understood the reasons. But Palmer would not control his destiny. Others had killed Chaz and others had brought him back to life. Now Chaz and Chaz alone determined his fate. He owned this body, sorry bag of bones that it was. Whatever happened from here on in would be Chaz's choosing.

He had not seen another vehicle for nearly 20 minutes when he came upon a Ford pickup truck. As evidenced by sharp, deep tracks that cut across the dirt, the truck had lost control and spun off the road. It rested a good 50 yards down the side of the canyon, badly battered from bouncing between the aspens and spruces like a pinball. The plummet had ended with a head first dive into an extra-large tree, bisecting the front hood.

Chaz pulled his motorcycle to the side of the road. Could someone be alive in that mess? He couldn't bring himself to speed off. He had to go down and see if there was anything he could do.

Chaz parked the bike and advanced on foot down the steep ridge, using the thick brush to control his descent. As he reached the smashed, red 4 x 4, he could see a lone occupant behind the wheel, face bloodied. A large, dead bull elk filled the back of the pickup, a hunting trophy that now had the last laugh. The elk's enormous antlers, one of the few things left unbroken by the accident, stretched out for the sky.

As Chaz got closer, he heard the man behind the wheel whimper.

Chaz responded, "Mister, don't move. I'll get help." It was an instinctive thing to say. Chaz had no cell phone, not that the reception would be any good out here.

"No use," muttered the man, a small spray of blood bouncing off his lips as he spoke. "I'm a goner."

"No, no," said Chaz, but upon a closer look at the man's condition, he knew it was true. The man, older with a thick beard and camouflage jacket, was bleeding profusely, filling a pool on the seat, barely able to lift his head.

"Please...put me out of my misery," said the man.

Chaz wanted to stop the bleeding but didn't know where to start. Then he saw the legs, horrifically bent at impossible angles, and he choked back a gasp.

"I'm suffering...please," said the man. Tears dribbled into the blood on his face. "The gun...in the back..." he said.

Chaz looked around, finding a scattered mess of hunting supplies. Then he saw it. A scoped, bolt-action rifle, the type used for big-game from long distances. While Chaz had friends who hunted, he was not a hunter himself. He couldn't imagine firing something like this point blank at a living man.

"I don't know...if I can," said Chaz, trying to extract the rifle from its entanglements.

"The small one," sputtered the hunter. "Hurry, please."

"Small one?" Then Chaz saw the second gun, sprung from its

case, a 7mm Magnum, surrounded by a spill of cartridges. This hunter had come prepared for close range and distance.

"Please," said the hunter. "Oh God, please."

Chaz reached into the truck, bringing his face in close proximity to the hunter's bloodied face, reaching past him for the Magnum.

Chaz had to control a sudden urge to lick the blood off the man's face.

He brought the gun out of the truck and inspected it for a moment. He looked back at the hunter. He was slumped over now, no longer conscious.

Dead?

Chaz looked him over carefully and could still see shudders coming from the man's chest. His eyelids flickered.

Chaz prepared the gun for a single shot to put the hunter out of his misery, granting him his final wish. He stood in the thick brush and aimed inside the cab of the truck.

He stared for a long moment at the dying man.

Then he dropped his arm. He couldn't shoot. Yet.

"Please forgive me," said Chaz out loud, and he wanted to cry at the hopelessness of the situation for both of them.

"I am so very sorry. But... I haven't had anything to eat in days."

The hunter just moaned a little. He probably could not imagine how his situation could get any worse.

But it did.

Chaz put aside the gun. His stomach growled. The impulses flooded over him and he knew it would be impossible to resist. The opportunity was too perfect.

As the glassy, dead eyes of the bull elk watched from the back of the pickup, Chaz feasted.

I am like any other animal on God's earth. I am feeding by instinct to survive. I cannot help myself. This is not a moral choice.

Chaz filled himself until he could consume no more, stuffing his face like it was Thanksgiving.

When he was done, he belched and granted the hunter his final wish. He shot him dead, a direct impact to the center of the brain, because as Chaz had learned, that was how you killed a zombie...or a victim of a zombie to prevent the curse from spreading.

The shot echoed across the canyon, sending a fluttering of birds out of the trees and soaring toward the heavens.

CHAPTER 16

The big, leafy spring colors of Wichita, Kansas, returned Chaz to his childhood. He had not been back in more than ten years, not since his parents passed away from different shades of cancer. He recalled how they lost control of their bodies to the inner invasion. He could now relate to their shock and fury as he himself turned slave to a wicked illness that ruled him like a cruel puppet master.

Chaz buzzed the Harley through familiar streets as memories poured at him from every direction. He truly felt like a ghost revisiting his past. So many of the homes remained unchanged, classic Midwestern residences with deep lawns and wide porches. He rode past the pale blue house he grew up in, two stories stacked in a square with a pitched roof, a pleasing flashback in time slightly jarred by new shutters and a satellite dish.

He circled his old high school, long and flat with little windows like a factory, still pumping out graduates every year to thrust upon adulthood.

A good chunk of the graduates went on to college, but not all. Chaz himself promptly joined the working world after high school—college was not an economic option. It meant a blue-collar career versus white, but one in construction that paid well. His reliable performance and versatility brought steady work, even during dips in the economy. He made good money.

Still, for his own son, Chaz pushed for higher aspirations. From the day Peter was born, Chaz contributed to a college savings fund that generated good returns, tax free, and swelled big to cover the equally big tuition costs. Peter chose Columbia University in New York among the many options offered by his strong academic record. He wanted to be a filmmaker and quickly demonstrated his talent by producing an award-winning short documentary on street gangs.

Peter's departure to begin his freshmen year was one of the proudest moments of Chaz's life. He had successfully advanced his son beyond his own humble beginnings.

Chaz ended his nostalgic trip through Wichita with a stop at Superior Autobody Repair on the outskirts of town. The faded sign and chipped paint out front greeted him with warm familiarity. Chaz parked his Harley under an oak tree. His ears filled with the whine of power tools and pounding of hammers against metal.

He walked past the technicians in the paint shop to peer into the main garage, a wide open space with a row of cars in various stages of repair. He glanced across faces until he found the familiar one: Frank Olsen. Chaz first met Frank when they played on the high school basketball team together and they became close, remaining in touch even as their lives took separate journeys.

Chaz knew Frank would help with a special request. He could trust Frank more than anyone. Chaz also craved a connection with another human being to make his own predicament less surreal. He wanted to exchange a few words with an old friend and regain some grounding in the living world.

Frank appeared in a state of deep concentration, and Chaz chose not to surprise him while he worked. Frank secured a smashed Toyota onto a loading ramp, attaching chains from the car to a hydraulic machine to pull the frame back into its proper position. He tightened a series of clamps and brackets, pausing only to wipe sweat from his forehead.

Chaz slipped into the body shop office where a rotund woman in a sleeveless, patterned shirt welcomed him. Framed certificates covered the wall behind her.

"I'm here to see Frank," said Chaz.

"Sure," said the woman. "Might be a few minutes. He's on a repair."

"No problem," said Chaz. He sat down in the small waiting area and buried his face in a fishing magazine.

Chaz rehearsed his greeting over and over in his head and realized there was no way his presence could not be outrageous and provoke any number of reactions—fear, anger, disbelief, even tears.

"Yo, someone lookin' for me?" came the unmistakable voice a few minutes later. Chaz looked up from the magazine to see Frank enter the office, wiping his oily hands on a rag. Aside from the continued retreat of his hairline, he looked more or less the same... the handsome power forward with the crooked nose from the high school basketball team.

"Hello, Frank," said Chaz. He stood up.

Frank faced the impossible. His head jerked back as if stunned by an illusion. His mouth opened to speak but stalled on the words. Finally, Frank spoke forcefully. "Do I *know* you?"

Chaz nodded.

Frank's hands tightened on the rag. "This is weird. You're not..."

Chaz nodded again.

"This isn't funny, man." Frank looked back at the fat woman behind the office counter, as if she might be in on the joke, but she was oblivious and buried in her schedule log, picking up the phone to make a call.

"I went to your funeral," said Frank in a hard but lowered voice.

Chaz shrugged and nodded again.

"Who are you *really*?" asked Frank.

Chaz spoke. "Can we meet somewhere? It's best we talk in private."

"You even sound like him," muttered Frank. He stepped closer, still staring. He reached out. He touched the fabric of Chaz's shirt.

"You're real."

"This isn't an acid flashback," said Chaz. "I'm really here, man."

Frank shook his head. "No. Okay. Listen. Whoever you are... I'll meet you in one hour at Corner Tavern. It's on..."

"I know where it is," said Chaz. "I grew up here, remember?"

"Shit," said Frank. "This is messed up."

**

One hour later, Frank met Chaz in a dim, back booth of Corner Tavern, away from the regulars who engaged in a raucous game of darts.

He slipped into the seat across from Chaz, still smudged with oil on his cheeks, extending not a greeting but a question.

"Sophomore year," said Frank. "Chaz and I went on a double date, bowling, with two hot chicks. Name them."

"Beth Nelson and Meg Evans," replied Chaz.

"Junior year, game against Wichita East, what happened in the second half?"

"You tripped over your shoelaces and I was laughing so hard I missed an easy shot. Coach McInally yelled at us for a month."

Frank scrunched his eyes shut, overcome by the absurdity of the encounter. He offered up one more.

"Algebra class. I needed a passing grade to avoid going into summer school and blowing up my entire summer. What happened?"

"Well," said Chaz. "I couldn't let you fail because your summer plans included me. We were going to spend all our time at the skateboard park. So we worked out a system. When you came to a question you weren't sure of, you dropped your pencil. That was the signal. I would look over, very discreetly, and then you would flash a series of fingers to identify the question. So halfway through the test, you dropped your pencil, I heard a *clunk*. I looked up, you flashed a one, and then a three. Question thirteen. That was a big one, like half the grade. So I gave you a signal back. We had devised a system where depending on where I touched, it coordinated to a number. If I rubbed my eye, a one. Touched my nose, a two. Tapped my lips, three. Stroked my chin, four..."

Frank continued: "Back of the head, five. Scratch your left shoulder, six. Scratch your right shoulder, seven..."

"Left leg, eight. Right leg, nine."

"And if you coughed, a zero!"

"So I looked at question 13 on my test. I knew I had the right answer. I touched my nose. I touched my chin. I scratched my left leg. And then..."

"You coughed," said Frank.

"2,480," said Chaz. "And you escaped the class with a passing grade, and we had the best summer of our lives."

Frank appeared dazed. "Why are you doing this to me? What happened, man? Am I dreaming?"

"That was my first reaction, too. I'm still getting used to this," said Chaz. He leaned closer. "Frank, I died. That really happened. But there was this secret experiment...it revived me. But everything is so screwed up... I don't know where to start."

A woman came by to take their drink orders.

Chaz sat back. "Water," he said.

"Bring me a very large Scotch," said Frank, hands trembling. "The sooner, the better."

**

Chaz told Frank everything, and it felt good to say it out loud, driving the madness from his head, watching someone else respond with horror and disbelief to confirm that he himself had not gone crazy.

Chaz stopped short of including one crucial fact: the hunger for human flesh. He wouldn't blame Frank if that little tidbit caused him to jump up and flee. Frank was already on edge and didn't need a push. The loyalty of this friendship had already been stretched to the limit.

Chaz finally revealed the big favor that waited in the wings.

"I have people after me," said Chaz. "So I can't stay in any one place for very long. I'm the last evidence of this experiment. And they want the evidence destroyed. So I've been riding across the country on my Harley, trying to stay one step ahead, but it's...it's really not safe. I can be traced to that bike, I'm wide open, I can't carry many supplies. At the body shop, do you still..."

Frank smiled and nodded. "Yes. I know where you're going with this." One of Frank's specialties was taking old junkers, fixing them up and selling them to used car lots. "I've got a couple of rehabs right now," he said.

Chaz said, "I need a car that is totally anonymous, doesn't have to be pretty but needs to be reliable and it can't be traced to me."

"Yeah," said Frank. "I can help you out. It's the least I can do to pay you back for 2,480."

"And you can do what you want with the Harley—sell it, dismantle it for parts. Just be sure to remove all traces of ownership."

"Easily done."

The waitress delivered their drinks. Chaz left his water untouched. Frank stared at his Scotch, let out a big sigh, grabbed the glass and took a hearty swallow.

After allowing the alcohol to settle his nerves, he said, "You can stay the night. I'm a bachelor these days. Tomorrow morning, we'll get your car. Might look like crap but I promise you one thing: It'll ride like a dream. I know, because I rebuilt the engine."

"Thanks," said Chaz, and he lifted his glass of water and clinked it to Frank's glass of Scotch. "To friendship."

"To friendship," echoed Frank, "through thick and thin, life and death."

CHAPTER 17

Chaz followed Frank to his house, driving a Volkswagen Jetta from the auto body shop, an even trade for the Harley. Windows open, he steered through the familiar, tree-lined streets, soaking in the calm. He felt closer to relaxed than any time since his rebirth. Nightfall rolled in like a comforting blanket.

Just before they reached Frank's house, a burst of ugliness blemished the tranquility. They passed a yard where a large, hairy man in a white t-shirt hollered at a gaunt woman with two small children.

Frank parked his souped-up Corvette in the driveway. Chaz pulled up alongside, parking the Jetta.

Now the neighbor's shouts could be heard loud and clear, an abrasive soundtrack to the picturesque setting.

"Fuck you! Fuck you!"

"Christ," muttered Frank. "There are little kids out there, for crying out loud."

Chaz stood on the driveway and watched the commotion two houses away.

The large hairy man took a step toward the woman, who let out a frightened squeak. Her children, a young son and even younger daughter, tucked themselves behind her.

"You will NOT tell me what to do. I do what I fucking please!" screamed the man, and he brought up a fist and waved it in the woman's face. She screamed, "Stop it! You're scaring the children."

"He better not..." said Chaz, stepping toward the scene.

"Hold on, you don't want to get mixed up in this," Frank told him.

"If he hits her..."

They watched the fireworks for a few more minutes. The man screamed and threatened. The woman finally ushered the children into the house. She shut the door on him, and he pounded on it for five minutes, BANG BANG BANG, like gunshots, until turning away in disgust.

He stormed back to his dented Chevy on the side of the road. He peeled away from the curb and roared off into the night.

"What an asshole," said Chaz.

"Yep," responded Frank. "Some things never change."

"What do you mean?"

"Don't you recognize him?"

Chaz said, "I don't know. He had his back to us."

"Bill Bledsoe."

The name struck Chaz like a bullet. "That's...Bledsoe?"

Frank sighed. "Yep. Lucky me. After spending high school with him beating the crap out of me, he moves in down the street."

"He used to terrorize me, too," said Chaz.

"And about half the class. Shit, that son of a bitch date raped a couple of chicks. One of them never recovered, it messed her up for life."

"What's the story with the woman?"

"That's his wife, Lora. Maybe ex-wife now. I know they're at least separated. He beats her, knocks around the kids."

"And the cops don't...?"

"His brother's on the force. Don't even bother going there."

"That's outrageous."

"Tell me about it. She kicked him out of the house. She tried getting a restraining order, but there's obviously not much restraint. He lives in a little apartment above the second hand store on Grove. Remember that place?"

"Sure."

Frank gave the house down the street one last look. "Well, he's gone. Show's over. Let's go in."

**

Chaz couldn't shake the bad memories stirred up by the reappearance of Bill Bledsoe. They sat in Frank's living room and pored over an old yearbook, revisiting the past. The recollections were tainted by the underlying tension of Bill Bledsoe, lurking unseen in the shadows of every photograph, like an evil spirit.

Bledsoe routinely picked on Chaz, forcing him into fights he did not want to engage in, fights that invariably left Chaz battered and bruised, and sometimes worse—at least one blackened eye and several bloody noses. Bledsoe typically fed on his victims for the sake of an audience to establish his dominance and build a personal mythology. The man was a renowned brute, compensating for a tiny brain with raw force utilized for the single purpose of sending a message: *I am superior to all of you.*

He was finally expelled during his junior year, hopeless at academics, but made it a habit to continue mixing with the students outside of school, causing ongoing destruction through mean-spirited vandalism and relentless bullying.

As Chaz flipped through the yearbook, Frank tried to steer the conversation back to happier times. But then Chaz came across a student photo that filled him with sadness.

Chaz stared into the eyes of Nicholas Gold, a small and sensitive kid who could never quite fit in with the rest of the class. Shy and awkward, Nicholas was largely ignored—except for the attention paid by Bill Bledsoe.

Bledsoe picked on Nicholas ruthlessly. Chaz had even tried to step in a few times and received a pummeling for interference.

On a rainy fall day, Nicholas hung himself, at age 15, a smart kid with an entire future ahead of him. While Bill Bledsoe couldn't be directly implicated, there was a common, unspoken understanding that he played a significant role in the youth's shattered confidence and empty self-esteem, instilling a sense of worthlessness that sought death over life.

**

Chaz slept on Frank's sofa; sleep defined as closing his eyes and lying very still. He sought a black void of unconsciousness but never truly drifted off, a curse of his condition. The relentless persistence of the real world, without relief from dreams and slumber, could only be described as true hell.

Ugly thoughts poked through his brain, revisiting the misery of his situation, and when he finally beat them back, a voice seeped into his head like the leader of all that was evil, taunting him from faraway.

"Fuck...you...you...piece...of...fucking...SHIT!"

Chaz sat up on the sofa.

He knew that voice. Bill Bledsoe.

The ogre had returned once more to terrorize the woman and two children down the street...at two a.m., no less. Perhaps the bars had closed and he needed fresh amusement.

Chaz walked over to the living room window and spread the heavy curtains for a look. Sure enough, the dented Chevy was back, half-parked on the lawn. The brute was planted on the front porch. Windows lit up the upper level of the house, but no one was going to invite this caller inside.

Bill Bledsoe hammered his thick fists on the door, sending another round of gunshot-like sounds across the neighborhood.

BANG BANG BANG

Chaz turned to glance at the closed door to Frank's bedroom. Frank slept. Just as well.

Chaz decided to go pay his old nemesis a visit. He no longer feared him. Chaz 1.0 was dead. Chaz 2.0 stood down for no one.

Chaz slipped out of the house and entered the night. He walked down the center of Birch Street toward Bledsoe like a cowboy stepping into a duel.

"Bledsoe!"

Bill Bledsoe turned from the door. He dropped his fists and squinted. "What the fuck?"

Chaz stood at the edge of the lawn, facing him. "Can't you see they want nothing to do with you?"

Bledsoe glowered. "Who the hell are YOU?"

"Chaz Singleton."

Bledsoe broke out in laughter—a strange sound coming from a man who rarely expressed anything but anger. "That's just fucked," he said.

He strolled over to Chaz. Chaz didn't move.

The two men stood a few feet apart, staring into one another's eyes. A gentle breeze rippled through the night.

Bledsoe lowered his voice, but it remained hard with menace. "You can't be him. I heard he died. I did a little dance when I heard the news."

"Did you wear a tutu?"

Bledsoe growled, "What did you do, fake your own death?"

"There's nothing fake about it."

"What's the matter with your skin?"

"I'm a zombie."

"Real funny. You always had a lot of zits. Wasn't that your nickname? Zitface, Pizza Face, you had so many names, I can't remember them all."

"I remember yours."

Bledsoe's eyes narrowed. "Oh yeah? What was it?"

"Shit for brains."

Bledsoe's response was swift. In the darkness, Chaz barely saw it coming, although it hardly surprised him. A fist struck his jaw with the force of a jackhammer and he landed in the grass just in time to receive a face full of boot.

After delivering a few more kicks, Bledsoe returned to his car. He revved up the engine but kept the headlamps off.

As Chaz sat up, he saw the Chevy roaring toward him. He made it to his feet but not out of the path of the car. It struck him hard. Chaz bounced off the front hood, catching a glimpse of Bledsoe's gleeful expression behind the windshield. Chaz's body spun and crashed back to the ground.

The Chevy tore across the yard, landed on the street and screeched into the distance.

Chaz lay on the grass, looking at the moon.

He felt no pain, only rage.

He rose to his feet. He brushed himself off.

He returned to Frank's house.

He rummaged through his travel bag, past the clothes and extra deodorant and cologne, until he touched metal.

Chaz pulled out the Magnum.

**

Chaz arrived at Second Time Around, the thrift shop located just around the corner from a main commercial strip of retail shops and restaurants, all shut down for the night except for the

24-hour convenience mart where he picked up a few items for his pending visit to an old acquaintance.

Chaz paused for a moment to stare into the window of Second Time Around. The musty shop had been the primary source for old toys and used comic books during his youth, well-meaning but frugal gifts from his parents, a constant reminder that their family had less money than most. Penny pinching was a daily necessity, always "Just a dry spell," until Chaz's father found more stable, better paying work, something that always seemed to elude him.

Still, Chaz grew to love those old toys and torn comic books.

Now he read the chipped, stenciled letters on the glass and realized they spoke to him more personally than ever.

This is my own second time around. And I'm going to take care of a few unresolved issues from my first time around.

Chaz opened a door on the side of the building and climbed a long flight of steps to a series of apartments stacked above the store. According to the shelf of mailboxes, Bledsoe resided in 2B.

Chaz knocked hard, his own version of Bledsoe's aggressive BANG BANG BANG.

After a long moment, a voice erupted raw and tired. "Who the *fuck* is it?"

"Pizza Face," replied Chaz.

Silence.

Then Bledsoe's voice returned, much closer to the door. "You gotta be shittin' me."

"I wasn't done talking with you."

"Yeah, well, I'm done with you."

"You weren't very nice."

Bledsoe struggled to reply. "I...you...what the fuck. Are you insane? Do you want another beating?"

"You're not so tough."

"So I have to teach you the same lesson twice? God damn it, you fucker..."

Bledsoe fumbled with the locks and threw open the door.

Chaz faced him with a gun pointed to his chest. In his other hand, he held a plastic bag of purchases.

Bledsoe's eyes grew big—not fearful but incredulous.

"You're going to shoot me?"

"No," said Chaz.

Bledsoe started to shut the door.

Chaz lunged forward, shoving the door open wider, knocking Bledsoe to one side.

Bledsoe stumbled back, stunned.

Chaz closed the door and faced his old enemy, still aiming the gun. "Take me to your kitchen."

"*What?*"

"You heard me."

"Why?"

"I'm hungry."

"You're crazy."

"No, I'm hungry."

Bledsoe scratched his armpit, shrugged and waved Chaz forward. "Okay. Come on."

Bledsoe still wore his white t-shirt, the jeans replaced with jockey shorts. "You woke me up," he muttered.

Chaz took in the surroundings, a mess of clutter and dopey indifference. Hardcore pornographic magazines littered tabletops, mingling with fast food wrappers.

"Nice bachelor pad you have here," said Chaz.

Bledsoe turned on the kitchen light, a bare bulb dangling over a small table next to a refrigerator and sink of dirty dishes.

"Now what? You want me to make you a sandwich?" growled Bledsoe.

"Sit in that chair." Chaz gestured with the gun.

"Why?"

Chaz aimed the gun at Bledsoe's head. "Or else."

Bledsoe sat down slowly, delivering a cold stare.

Chaz reached into his sack and brought out a long rope. "Hope I remember my knots from Boy Scouts."

"Fuck you, you fucker."

"Do you know *any* other words?"

Chaz tied Bledsoe to the chair, binding his wrists behind his back and his ankles to the chair legs.

"You gotta tie me up before you shoot me?" said Bledsoe. "Be a man, shoot me now."

"I told you, I'm not going to shoot you," said Chaz. He finished the final knot and pulled tight to ensure Bledsoe couldn't go anywhere.

"Then what? You gonna tell me a bedtime story?"

Chaz turned away and began browsing through Bledsoe's cabinets and drawers. He found what he was looking for: a plate and some utensils. He brought them over to the kitchen table and sat across from Bledsoe. He began to empty the remaining items from his sack.

Bledsoe watched with great interest.

A bottle of ketchup. A salt shaker. A large bib. A fork. An electric carving knife.

Chaz put on the bib. He plugged the carving knife into a wall socket.

"Do you remember Susan Knipp?" asked Chaz.

Bledsoe's eyes locked on the carving knife. "Susan...who?"

"The girl you date raped when she was fifteen."

"That was... She was... fuck you!"

Chaz's thumb flicked the carving knife to life. It emitted a steady hum. "This is for Susan," said Chaz.

Chaz leaned forward. He sliced off a piece of Bledsoe's arm. Bledsoe screamed, blood spurted. Chaz brought the pink chunk of flesh to his plate. He added a little salt and ketchup, stabbed it with his fork and gobbled it down as Bledsoe watched, mortified.

"Ordinarily, I'm not into greasy fast food," said Chaz as he chewed. "But I'm so damned hungry that tonight I'll make an exception."

Bledsoe began hollering.

Chaz stood up, found an old dish rag by the sink and used it to gag him, muffling his cries.

Then Chaz sat back down.

"Do you remember how you picked on your cousin Ricky, framing him for a crime that you yourself committed? I hear he's serving 20 years, the poor thing. This is for little Ricky."

Chaz revved up the carving knife and cut loose another slice of Bledsoe. He chewed on it slowly, shutting his eyes and savoring the flavor, while Bledsoe's smothered screams filled the room.

Every bite was preceded by a story. "I hear you hit your eight-year-old daughter...told the authorities she ran into a door...clever, but nobody buys that." He cut off Bledsoe's ear and chomped on it like a potato chip.

"Remember Nicholas Gold? You destroyed that poor boy. You sentenced him to death. And the only thing he was guilty of was being weaker than you."

Chaz brought the vibrating blade to Bledsoe's fat belly and cut through the t-shirt to get a big chunk of the main course. The gag absorbed Bledsoe's eruption of agony. Then his head began to dip, woozy.

Chaz said, "In a minute I'm going to empty your jugular vein so I have something to wash all this down with. You got any glasses?"

Chaz dug through the kitchen cabinets until he found a plastic tumbler with a happy clown face, a freebie from a local hamburger joint. "You don't have any nice wine glasses? Guess not. I'm afraid this will have to do."

Every victim from Bledsoe's long history of abuse was honored with their own piece of their tormentor's dying body. After Bledsoe passed out for good, Chaz gave way to his undead impulses. He pushed aside the eating utensils and feasted directly on Bledsoe with his teeth, tearing into him like a meaty chicken bone.

Chaz satisfied his hunger, reducing Bledsoe to a partial human being, missing pieces all over his body. When the bully lurched back to existence as a zombie, his physical coordination was laughably clumsy, flopping about like a broken wind-up toy expelling energy with no coordinated movements.

Chaz retrieved a large cushion from the living room sofa and brought it into the kitchen. He placed it over zombie Bledsoe's face and pointed the end of the Magnum at the portion of the cushion covering Bledsoe's forehead. He fired once, a direct hit to the brain and Bledsoe died for the second time that evening.

"Sorry for the mess," muttered Chaz, dropping the burst cushion to the floor, observing how the kitchen's dirty white color had turned a splashy red.

Chaz cleaned up. He left the apartment and returned to

Frank's house. He quietly slipped in through the front door, not wanting to bother his friend.

Before retiring to a satisfied semi-sleep, Chaz visited the bathroom to floss his teeth and swirl mouthwash in the back of his throat.

**

The next morning, Chaz packed his modest belongings and thanked Frank for the visit, the automobile and the kind acceptance of his outrageous new state of existence.

"You are a true friend," said Chaz. "You accept me for what I am, even when it's not what you bargained for."

"I don't pretend to understand it," said Frank. "But I want the best for you, man, whatever that may be."

"I'd hug you..." said Chaz. "But I'm sort of contagious."

Frank smiled. "Understood."

A peaceful calm hung over Birch Street. No shouts came from the Bledsoe house down the block. Under a sparkling sun, Chaz drove off in the old red Jetta, giving one last look to his friend in the rearview mirror.

**

Frank watched the Jetta disappear around the corner and returned inside his house. The living room held a pungent odor, a lingering reminder of his friend's sickness. He opened the windows for a rush of clean air. Then he headed for the shower to get ready for a new day at the auto body shop. He was running late.

After cleaning up and drying down, Frank stepped out of the bathroom. He never made it to the bedroom. A man stood crouched in the hallway, aiming an assault rifle. Frank jumped, startled. The man fired twice.

Frank Olsen dropped to the rug, dead within seconds.

**

Breck Palmer checked to make sure Frank Olsen had not only died but did not display any bite marks that would indicate zombie infection. He peeled away the bath towel, looked him over, and felt satisfied that this corpse would not get back up.

Even so, he shot him one more time in the head.

Palmer quickly exited the house and climbed into his white van, a mobile assassin's headquarters. The van held a heavy load of weapons, computers and communication equipment to aid in the tracking and destruction of Chaz Singleton and any witnesses and victims in his wake. With all the high-tech resources at his disposal, the clue that led Palmer to the home of Frank Olsen had actually been very simple: Chaz Singleton's battered old address book, personally pulled by Palmer from a desk drawer in Chaz's home back in Tucson. It held the names and locations of everyone Chaz knew, a convenient listing of potential destinations and accomplices in the getaway flight of the last zombie on earth.

CHAPTER 18

Chaz traveled hundreds of miles across the Midwest, a rolling sprawl of flat terrain and billboards, only stopping to refuel and give the old car a rest. He required little rest himself and continued to make great time, reaching the outskirts of Indianapolis after dark. He kept close to the speed limit, driving steady and focused behind the wheel. Getting into an accident or stopped by the highway patrol would invite disaster.

When light rain splashed against the windshield, it loosened the layers of dirt and dust into a smeary film. Chaz operated the windshield wipers and discovered he was out of wiper fluid. Just as well—the Jetta could use a short break and he should stretch his legs even if they were too numb and deadened to signal pain and fatigue.

He took the next off-ramp and entered a dense cluster of lights: a hub for travelers, consisting of fast food chains, gas stations, motels and a mini mart.

He entered the bumpy parking lot for the mini mart and snapped off the engine, which shuddered and sighed before shutting down.

Chaz checked his reflection in the rear view mirror: bloodshot eyes, pale skin, dull face. Hopefully he looked no different than any other weary traveler.

His mouth was dry and sticky, and although he didn't feel thirsty, he knew he could use some water. If nothing else it would loosen up his articulation if he had to speak to someone.

Chaz entered the mini mart, triggering a cheerful jingle. He glanced at the cashier and customer at the front counter.

Right away, he could tell something was wrong.

The little old woman behind the counter stood stiff with hands raised halfway, palms out, big eyes magnified and unblinking behind thick glasses.

The stubble-headed man in the trench coat facing her held something under his coat that protruded in her direction. He gave Chaz a quick, startled frown and Chaz immediately realized he had walked in on a robbery.

"Stop right where you are," said the man. The dark stubble peppered his scalp and face like dirt.

Chaz continued walking forward.

"Stop!" shouted the man, and he pulled his hand out from under the trench coat to reveal the pistol in his grasp.

Chaz advanced. "Leave that woman alone," he said.

"If you take another step—!" shouted the man.

Chaz kept walking straight at him.

"Back off!" shouted the man, and then he fired the pistol twice. The clerk screamed.

Chaz felt two bee stings in his chest, mild nuisances that didn't slow his advance.

When the robber saw Chaz continuing to come at him, his eyes bulged even wider than the terrified expression on the clerk. He fired one more shot, but this time his hand trembled so bad that it missed its target and exploded a bottle of Gatorade.

Chaz grabbed two pots of steaming coffee from the counter, one in each hand, and splashed them forward at the robber, smacking his face with the scalding liquid. As he screamed, Chaz struck him twice in the head, once with each pot, shattering both, and the man crumpled to the floor unconscious in a pool of coffee, broken glass and blood.

The old woman behind the counter remained frozen in fear, a tiny head of gray hair and big glasses, wearing a red smock with a nametag reading "Marge."

Chaz bent down, took the robber's gun and handed it to her.

"Here. Keep this away from him. Call the police. I think he'll be out for a while."

The woman just nodded, speechless.

Then Chaz shopped for the windshield wiper fluid and bottled water. He paid for his purchases, stepping over the fallen robber.

The clerk, still petrified, managed a stammering "Th-th-thank you."

"My pleasure," said Chaz, departing from the mart, and he meant it.

**

Chaz put considerable distance between himself and the mini mart before rolling off the highway early the following morning to take care of the foreign objects in his body.

He found a random pancake house with a tall sign and wide parking lot crowded with trucks. A good place to be anonymous for a few minutes.

Chaz bypassed the tables of greasy breakfasts and a long counter of tired souls hunched over coffee mugs. He headed into the bathroom, entered a stall, secured the door and sat on the toilet lid.

Chaz unbuttoned his shirt, torn and stained from the bullets. As during prior attacks on his person, the bleeding did not last long, clotting quickly.

He reached under his shirt for the sheath attached to his belt and extracted a knife.

Chaz cut into his chest carefully, with precision, around the first bullet, loosening the flesh, causing a little bleeding, poking until he found his target. Then, as if picking out a splinter, he extracted the bullet.

It landed on the floor with a clatter that echoed off the dirty tiles.

He cut into his chest a second time, digging for the next bullet. He inserted the blade beneath it and pushed on the handle until the bullet popped out.

"Aaah," said Chaz. "Now that's better." He wiped his chest with toilet paper and flushed it. He buttoned up and left the stall, washing his hands before exiting the restroom.

As Chaz made his way past the long counter of coffee drinkers, he heard something that caused him to stop in his tracks.

On a television screen hoisted above, a news anchor reported on a convenience store robbery just outside Indianapolis.

Shit, thought Chaz, and he turned to look.

A fuzzy, greenish clip played in slow motion, showing the

robber firing two bullets into a man who barely flinched. A graphic at the bottom of the screen read: *Security Camera Footage.*

The clip continued, capturing the coffee pot attack and Chaz handing the gun to the elderly clerk. After a jump cut, the footage showed Chaz calmly purchasing windshield wiper fluid and bottled water.

The news anchor continued: "After being shot twice at close range, the man made his purchases and continued on his way. Local police are calling him a 'mystery hero,' and anyone with information about his identity is encouraged to contact authorities. The store owners want to personally thank him and pay for his medical treatment. Area hospitals are on the alert."

The television replayed the clip of the robber's gun firing at Chaz, two quick flashes. The anchor said, "Officials studying the footage are at a loss to describe how anyone could withstand such a shooting. The mystery hero is quickly becoming a national celebrity, and when we know more about his identity, we will be sure to share it with you."

"That feller is a gol-darned SUPER hero," spoke up a wrinkly old man on a stool at the coffee counter. "Those bullets bounced off a him like Superman."

A beefy trucker in a red cap nodded in agreement. "Did you see how he kept comin' after that bastard? Sheeit."

Chaz turned away from the television monitor, stared down at the ground and made a hasty exit from the pancake house.

**

Breck Palmer sat in the back of the white van, surrounded by his guns, computers and communication equipment, viewing the security camera footage frame by frame on a small monitor.

There was no doubt in his mind that the "mystery hero" was Chaz.

"You can run, but you can't hide, my zombie friend," said Palmer.

He stepped out of the van, which sat parked in front of the now famous Indianapolis mini mart, surrounded by media trucks from every major network.

Palmer stood off to the side as reporters interviewed the old lady cashier, over and over with the same questions. She looked like she hadn't slept since the episode occurred and still couldn't believe the chain of events.

"What would you say to your mystery hero if he was here with you today?" asked a female reporter with a hard voice and soft face.

"I would say...thank you," responded the old woman as tears began to fill her tired eyes. "Thank you and God bless you, mister, whoever you are."

When Palmer finally got his turn with her, he told the elderly cashier, "I'm not a reporter. I only have a few questions. I'm with...the FBI," he lied.

Palmer produced a small color photo of Chaz Singleton, shielding it from anyone else's view. He showed it to the woman and spoke in a quiet tone. "Is this your mystery hero?"

"Yes." The woman grew excited. "Yes, that's him. Do you know him?"

Palmer signaled for her to lower her voice. "We might. Do you know where he was headed?"

"I have no idea."

"Did he say anything to you? What were his exact words?"

"Just to call the police. And to keep the change."

"Did he bite anyone?"

The old woman stared at him. "What?"

"Bite. With his teeth. Did he bite anyone? Did he bite the holdup man?"

"No," said the old woman.

"Are you sure?"

"Yes, I'm sure. What an odd question." She turned away from Palmer. "I'm tired. I've been talking to reporters all day. I want to sit down."

Palmer thanked her.

He returned to his van. He pulled up a mapping system on the computer. A red line showed the path of Chaz Singleton, starting in Tucson, advancing to the location of the dead hunter in the New Mexico mountains, then moving to Wichita, followed by a connection to the mini mart on the outskirts of Indianapolis. Chaz was making his way northeast across the country.

Palmer knew his role was not only to stop Chaz Singleton but to be his cleaning crew. He had to "mop up" after Chaz to make sure none of his victims spread the plague. He constantly monitored traditional and social media for news of any bite victims or the slightest hint of cannibalism.

Fortunately, Chaz appeared to understand the dangers of his infection and proactively shot his meals in the head. However, the risk remained that he could get sloppy, and his mind might deteriorate into a state shared by the basic zombies where flesh-eating took over without a conscience about consequences.

The safest thing for the world was the destruction of Chaz Singleton. Perhaps Chaz felt he deserved special treatment as a "smart zombie," but the risks of letting him exist outweighed anything else.

The appearance in Indianapolis helped to confirm Palmer's suspicions of Chaz's ultimate destination. He had seen the name and address in Chaz's address book and deemed the subject a likely target, almost too likely.

Chaz's son, Peter Singleton, attended school at Columbia University in New York City.

Palmer knew he had to head off Chaz's arrival in Manhattan, because the risk of introducing the virus to the biggest city in the country was unthinkable.

If the zombie plague erupted and spread across New York, that would surely be the beginning of the end.

CHAPTER 19

The hunger consumed him, blazing in his belly and raging through his brain.

Chaz Singleton needed to eat.

He knew he would merely spit up normal food. He had succumbed to his grotesque nutritional needs. Two questions remained: where...and *who?*

As he drove through Pittsburgh, a big metropolis on his route to Manhattan, everyone looked tasty, clothing serving as candy wrappers that needed to be torn away to reveal the yummies inside.

Chaz knew these thoughts were sick but it didn't stop him from obsessing over them.

The gun remained in its holster, equipped with only a few more bullets. He thought about the strange reversal at play—how hunters shot and ate their prey, but Chaz ate his food first and then shot it.

He drove the Jetta through Pittsburgh's hilly terrain, two-way lanes on steep slopes curving through gentrified neighborhoods.

He wanted to limit his feedings to individuals who deserved elimination, evil doers harmful to society like the awful Bill Bledsoe.

He toyed with the idea of breaking into a prison and feasting on criminals like a big buffet, but the same forces that kept them in would keep him out.

His eyes roamed his surroundings, knuckles tight on the wheel. He felt taunted by flesh packaged in every shape, size, color and flavor.

Then he drove past a modest, pink building that offered a possibility he could not shake, resulting in a screeching U-turn.

What about food that remained on the shelf past its expiration date?

Chaz pulled up in front of Heritage Manor, a nursing home. The old brick facility appeared sad and tired, reflecting its occupants.

Chaz thought hard. These people were already on their way out. They had lived good, long lives. At this point, they were just hanging on. Maybe he could find someone fading and comatose where death would be a blessing?

He knew his musings were insane but the hunger gripped him and took over any rational thought.

Chaz pulled away from the curb. He drove a few blocks further to a small shopping district. He found a florist, parked and purchased a big, bright bouquet.

Chaz left his car in the lot and walked back to the nursing home, not wanting his getaway car and license plate too close to the scene of the impending crime.

Before he entered Heritage Manor, he looked heavenward, offering a part prayer, part apology to God. However, it didn't feel right, given that Chaz was surely well beyond forgiving. He had already died and gone to Hell.

Getting past the bored front desk receptionist merely required waving the flowers and speaking in a casual tone. "I'm back to see Uncle Ernie," he announced, keeping the bouquet in front of his face. The receptionist began to say something—perhaps a request for him to sign in—but halted and let him go when his confident pace continued down the corridor.

Chaz began looking in rooms for the ideal candidate—someone who would not lose too many days of life if their death was accelerated.

As it turned out, that criteria fit a lot of the occupants. Even the ones who were not bedridden staggered around with lost eyes, pale faces and dim thoughts like a colony of the undead.

These people look more like zombies than I do, thought Chaz.

Up ahead, he saw a doctor and nurse exiting one of the patient rooms.

"I give her three days, tops," said the doctor, and the nurse nodded in agreement.

Chaz realized he had found his ideal candidate. He waited for them to disappear from view and then entered the room.

He shut the door behind him and placed the flowers on a table.

He looked at the withered old woman in the bed, a sickly continuity of gray from her skin to her hair, as if someone had erased all evidence of color.

Her eyes were shut, the mouth drooped open.

A hand wrapped in veins and age spots held the bed sheet.

Not the most appetizing spread but beggars can't be choosers, he thought to himself.

Chaz realized an unusual sensation in his mouth—wetness. He was salivating.

Chaz readied his plan: eat quickly, then place a pillow over her face, shoot the brain and escape out the window.

He wished he had brought ketchup or mustard, something to help with the inevitable dryness of this particular meat. Maybe she had some condiments handy?

He began to look around, then stopped and told himself, *you're procrastinating, so get on with it!*

Chaz leaned over the old woman...

She opened her eyes.

Chaz gasped and pulled back.

The old woman also gasped, a hoarse wheeze.

Chaz fled the room.

In the corridor, a man in a green orderly's smock caught his panicked pace and came toward him. "Hey, sir, do you have a visitor's badge?"

"Yes," said Chaz, turning away in the opposite direction.

"Can you show it to me?"

"No." Chaz broke out in a trot.

The orderly called out: "Security!"

Chaz ran. He took a sharp turn down another corridor and found an emergency exit.

He slammed through the door and spilled into an alley. He ran from the nursing home, slipping between another set of buildings. After several twists and turns, he stumbled behind an office complex and hid behind a large green dumpster.

Chaz waited and listened. He heard nothing. Quite possibly, no one had bothered to pursue him outdoors.

"Hep me wif sumfin to eat?" came a sudden, rough voice.

Chaz jumped and spun around.

A filthy, bearded homeless man approached in off-balance, toddler-like steps, his hand extended.

"No," said Chaz, "but I could ask you the same question."

"Y'got money?"

"I'm running low on cash and I need to see my son," Chaz replied, matter of fact. "I'm sorry..."

"I jus' need ten dollars."

Chaz began to walk away. The homeless man followed, his voice growing more persistent. "You haf money? I need ten dollars. Okay, nine."

Chaz kept his back to the man, simply wanting to discontinue the conversation, but the move left him open to a surprise attack.

Chaz felt something strike him in the back of the head and crumpled to the dirt and weeds. Disoriented and weak from hunger, he struggled to get back on his feet and then the homeless man came at him again, gripping a lead pipe, bloodshot eyes bulging, exclaiming, "Mudder fugger!"

The next blow crashed across Chaz's forehead—his one area of vulnerability, the brain that kept the rest of him functioning like a battery pack.

"No! Stop it!" screamed Chaz, but the homeless man had turned vicious and desperate. When the next blow landed, Chaz erupted into a rage.

Leaping at the bum, Chaz's inner animal instincts took over. He bit his attacker on the arm and the man hollered, dropping the pipe. The flesh tasted so good that Chaz knew there was no stopping now...

He took a chomp out of the bum's neck.

The bum screamed and began running. Chaz pursued him across a vacant lot. The bum headed toward a large steel bridge that spanned one of Pittsburgh's three rivers. He scampered up a gravel incline into a narrow crawl space where the bridge met the earth. Chaz watched him slip inside a tattered cardboard box like a gopher returning to its hole. As the bum entered, several chubby rats scurried out.

Chaz followed into the box.

The bum wedged himself in the corner of his dark, tiny home, a nest of blankets, plastic bags and newspapers. Bright red blood bubbled from his neck like a fountain beckoning to quench the thirst of a man who hadn't seen a drink in days.

Chaz feasted.

When he was done eating, he pulled his gun out of its holster. The homeless man had passed out after the first few bites but now it was necessary to put him in a permanent sleep and not spread the zombie virus.

Chaz waited for the thick rumble of a truck on the bridge overhead to cover the gunshot. In no time at all, a booming truck arrived, shaking the bridge and the earth beneath it, and Chaz shot the bum between the eyes.

As Chaz began to extract himself from the dirty, cramped space, he knocked past several clinking bottles.

He glanced down.

Jack Daniels. Jim Beam.

Holy shit.

They were empty. Chaz realized he was growing very dizzy.

He backed out of the cardboard box and crawled away from the bridge. As he stood, he immediately endured a nasty head rush.

Chaz nearly fell down.

He took several steps and could barely keep his balance. He threw out his arms, prepared for a fall.

His thoughts swam around and around, disjointed and sloppy, as if...

I'm drunk, realized Chaz.

He looked back at the homeless man's headquarters. *The old fool was bombed on booze. I ate a meal soaked in alcohol.*

That explained the rather nasty taste, which he had originally written off to lack of bathing.

Chaz staggered away from the bridge, the traffic overhead now extra loud, pounding and throbbing inside his skull. He wanted to throw up. He jammed fingers down his throat but nothing happened, and in his inebriated state he almost chewed on his own hand.

The blue sky above began spinning and Chaz fought to remain on his feet. He growled, swore, and hated himself as an expanding fog rolled into his brain.

I'm wasted.

CHAPTER 20

Chaz awoke, staring into a disorienting texture that turned out to be the ceiling of the Volkswagen Jetta. He shifted in the back seat. Through the windows, he could see portions of the Pittsburgh shopping strip that included the flower shop where he bought the nursing home bouquet.

Is it early morning? Late afternoon?

He had no memory of the past few—or perhaps many—hours. A big eraser had wiped his recollections clean.

All he knew was that he had crawled into the backseat of his car and slipped into a rare unconsciousness.

Also one other thing: his belly was very full.

Chaz touched his stomach under the shirt and it felt stretched, as if he had consumed half a dozen Thanksgiving dinners.

"Oh no," he groaned.

He saw blood on his shirt, on the backs of his hands, and felt a crust around his mouth.

After the hobo...where did I go, what did I do? wondered Chaz.

He forced his stupid zombie brain to *think, think, think.*

Faint memories surfaced, one by one, a sequence of attacks under the darkness of night.

A skanky prostitute in torn fishnet stockings...a roaming, rotund derelict looking to score drugs...a wandering, club-hopping teen.

They all tasted so good.

Holy shit, I got drunk and went on an eating binge!

He checked the chamber of his gun and it confirmed his worst fears: he had not fired any shots after the bullet for the homeless man.

He had not taken proper care of his subsequent victims, which meant...

"Oh no, no, no, no..." he muttered to himself.

He sat up and quickly changed his bloody shirt for a clean one in his travel bag. He scrubbed at the blood stains on his face and hands with a sanitary wipe.

As he hurried to clean himself, he heard a siren tear into the air.

Oh God, this is a nightmare inside of a nightmare.

Chaz opened the car door and stepped out. He tracked the siren to a police car, catching sight of the passing flash of red lights. After making a turn, the vehicle pulled up next to an ambulance and another police car parked in front of a tall building. A small crowd filled the sidewalk.

Chaz reached back into the Jetta and grabbed a hoodie and pair of sunglasses. He put them on to conceal his identity and then headed for the growing commotion.

Chaz arrived just in time to see paramedics emerge from an alley with a body on a gurney. From the shape of the lump under the sheet, Chaz guessed it was the drug seeker.

Chaz seamlessly blended in with the rest of the onlookers and watched as the gurney split a path through the crowd, moving slowly toward the rear of the ambulance.

Without warning, a sudden BANG erupted like a firecracker, and several people squealed. Then one of the squeals turned into a full-blooded scream and more screams joined in.

A stain of red appeared at the head of the wrapped body on the gurney, spreading across the sheet. The paramedics scrambled for cover. Two policemen pulled out their guns and twirled, trying to find the source of the shot.

Chaz looked upward and caught a quick glimpse of a figure on a nearby rooftop. The split-second view was all Chaz needed to make an identification. The gunman was Breck Palmer.

Palmer had no doubt heard about the overnight murders with cannibalism overtones and raced to the scene to prevent the virus from spreading.

Chaz felt grateful—and terrified. His mistakes were being corrected but his existence was in jeopardy. He deduced Palmer had not seen him in the crowd, because if he had, Chaz would have been the first target.

The scene at the foot of the building grew chaotic as the crowd scattered in all directions. Additional police arrived. Chaz walked swiftly back to his car. He had to leave Pittsburgh immediately and continue on his journey to see Peter.

Nothing would prevent him from seeing his son, not even this debacle.

Peter was the only sane thing left in Chaz's life, the lone inspiration that kept him from putting a bullet in his own skull.

Chaz drove the Jetta onto the Pennsylvania turnpike. He left Pittsburgh in the rearview mirror and continued to his destination.

CHAPTER 21

Breck Palmer seethed with anger. He drove the unmarked white van through the winding streets of Pittsburgh, swearing at the man who eluded him and now threatened to destroy civilization with his carelessness.

Palmer had predicted it all: Dr. Rabe's prized "smart zombie" would inevitably grow stupid and sloppy as his dumb, raw instincts took over. You could not trust an advanced zombie race. At the core, they were all savages. Palmer would kill every last one of them, single-handedly if necessary.

He remembered the early days of the experiment and the dreams of a controlled species of resilient, obedient, expendable super soldiers.

Not only had they failed at strengthening America's military might against the rest of the globe, now there was a serious threat of bringing down the country from within.

The Pittsburgh police radio crackled over the van's speakers, providing real-time updates on Chaz's victims. So far, three late night snacks had been identified. Palmer secured the permanent demise of two of them through sniper shots from nearby building rooftops, direct hits to the head before they made it to the morgue.

This ignited chaos and resulted in a much larger police presence at the crime scene of the third victim, a middle-aged prostitute found stuffed in a trash can.

Palmer had to save his bullet to the brain for a less public, more manageable space: the Allegheny County Medical Examiner's Office.

As he pulled up to the nondescript, single-level building, he saw several police cars parked out front.

The morgue was being guarded.

No one knew why a crazy man was on the loose shooting murder victims who were already dead, but they weren't going to let it happen again.

Palmer prepared to face armed resistance. He parked the van and gathered a small arsenal: tear gas to create confusion, a gas mask to protect himself, and three guns. He threw on a large jacket to cover it all and stepped out of the vehicle.

Prepared for a violent confrontation, Palmer stepped into the office lobby, fingers just inches from the quick release of a snub nose .45.

Nothing happened. The lobby was eerily quiet, no police presence, no clerk.

Palmer advanced toward the morgue in the back. He nearly stumbled over a body on the ground.

Palmer stared down at the open, glassy eyes of a dead policeman, face paralyzed in fear, a fatal chunk bitten out of his neck.

"Shit," said Palmer softly. He was too late.

He hurried into the autopsy room, passing another dead policeman. In the examination bay, he found a gurney flipped over and a sprawling mess of spilled lab utensils and broken X-ray equipment.

Two limp bodies lay in humps nearby, wearing gloves, face masks and hairnets. Palmer inspected them—one appeared to be a staff autopsy technician, the other a forensic investigator—both dead with unmistakable bite marks.

Splattered blood still dripped in streaks down the stainless steel cabinets.

These were fresh kills and it was only a matter of time before another round of police entered the space.

Palmer knew what he had to do.

He shot each of the four victims in the head.

As he stood over the last victim, a young policeman, he felt sick inside. This man probably had a wife and kids, and his life had been wasted, turned into zombie food. In what twisted universe did living beings make a meal out of another life?

For a brief moment, he recognized the hypocrisy of his compassion. Palmer swore on the spot to become a vegetarian. Then he doubted he could ever hold himself to it. He loved a good hamburger.

Palmer watched the growing pool of blood beneath the policeman's head, the bullet hole pumping a steady flow like a tap.

"God forgive me," he whispered.

Palmer turned to leave.

A zombie woman with bulging eyes and a gaping mouth lunged at him.

Palmer screamed. Her hands clutched him and her teeth clattered with hunger. He shoved her back and she staggered in high heels.

By the look of her business attire and name tag, this was probably the lobby receptionist, the official in charge of logging in pathologists, toxicologists, law enforcement officials, next of kin and corpses. She had now joined the latter.

With raw force, she lunged again at Palmer. He fought to position his gun at her head, but she was too close, too spasmodic, and it took all of his energy to peel her off. He heard her jaws chomp just inches from his nose, her face huge and crazed in front of him. She felt no pain from his punches and grabbed his throat with a vice-like grip, like a wild animal digging claws into its prey.

Palmer could smell the rancid stench of her dead breath blasting into his face.

BLAM

Her left eye exploded, replaced by a socket of runny red and white, and she stumbled back several steps in her high heels, finally toppling to the floor, hands twitching.

BLAM

One more shot to seal the deal, and her forehead popped open a spray of blood with an impressive arc across the lobby.

Palmer shuddered. He quickly checked himself for bite marks, scratches or potential infection of any kind. He found none.

He hurried outdoors, where his ears immediately detected distant sirens. He climbed into the van and peeled out of the parking lot as fast as possible. The sirens increased in volume and layers, a team of police just minutes away from a most gruesome discovery at the medical examiner's office.

**

As night fell, dropping darkness on Pittsburgh, Palmer drove through the city streets, up, down and across, listening to the police scanner. At least one zombie remained on the loose: the dead prostitute who escaped from the morgue. If she had bitten anyone, then the number of zombies would grow exponentially very quickly and could become impossible to contain.

The police radio buzzed nonstop with chatter about the slaughter at the morgue, everybody was wildly confused by the cannibalism attacks combined with sniper shootings combined with a missing corpse.

None of it made sense to anyone, except to Palmer.

On his fifth hour of prowling Pittsburgh, he finally discovered what he was looking for and nearly shouted out loud with excitement and relief.

A dirty, disheveled woman staggered like a sleepwalker down a shadowy sidewalk on the opposite side of the street. She had streaky blonde hair, smeared lipstick, a halter top, torn fishnet stockings and no shoes.

The "dead giveaway" was the morgue tag still attached to her toe.

Palmer grabbed for a rifle with one hand and yanked the steering wheel with the other, pulling an immediate, screeching U-turn.

He brought the van closer to the zombie woman, slowing the vehicle to a crawl, steadying his gun for a shot to the head.

"Shit," said Palmer. He realized the woman's mouth was not smeared with lipstick—it was smeared in blood. She had been feeding.

That meant more victims...creating more victims.

Palmer had a perfect shot lined up and then the zombie abruptly turned and entered a bar, Harvey's Tavern.

"Damn it, damn it, damn it!" Palmer accelerated to the first open space against the curb. He parked the van and exchanged the rifle for a handgun. Now he was going to have to enter the tavern, where things were going to get much more complicated very quickly.

He stepped inside and immersed himself in the crowd. Loud rock music and shouting voices filled his ears. The lights were very low, save for occasional neon beer logos. Palmer had to wait for his eyes to adjust before he could discern any faces. He moved through the throng, pushing his way forward when necessary, receiving some glares.

Suddenly, he saw two entangled shadows in a corner, a woman feeding on a struggling man. Palmer drew his gun, rushing at them, prepared to stop the assault with a single bullet...

But then he realized it was not a zombie attack. This was merely a young couple making out, the woman kissing with uninhibited aggression and the man roaming his hands across her breasts. They looked like they were chewing on one another, but it was just two horny kids.

Palmer heard a crash and swung around to face another part of the bar. He saw a staggering, awkward human shape pushing through the crowd, jarring drinks out of the hands of patrons in its path.

Zombie! screamed Palmer's brain. He again prepared for a clean shot to the head, but then the figure emerged from the shadows and it was just a stupid drunk. His clumsy, inebriated steps resembled the walking dead, but this was not the flesh-eating variety.

As Palmer continued to circle the bar, he became more frustrated. The zombie woman was nowhere in sight. How could that be? Had she slipped out the back? But why? She had encountered a smorgasbord of human flesh without a nibble? It didn't make sense.

Then he heard a loud drunk man near him exclaim, "I gotta pee!" At that moment, Palmer realized there was still one place left unchecked.

Palmer raced the "gotta pee" man to the men's room and entered first. He found no cause for alarm: just a lone dude at a urinal, an empty toilet stall and a messy sink.

Palmer advanced to the women's bathroom, prepared with an "Oops! Sorry! Thought this was the men's room!" if it was occupied with ordinary patrons.

He twisted the handle, but the door didn't budge.

Locked from the inside.

Palmer had no idea what was taking place inside but the risk of leaving the space unexplored was too much.

The bar music pounded and throbbed, a useful cover for the sound of his shoulder against the door, slamming hard and breaking it open.

Palmer stumbled into total darkness. His hands roamed for the light switch. He felt a tiny bump against the wall and flipped it. The small room illuminated in a bright splash of light.

The zombie prostitute sat on the tile floor, gnawing on the limp bare arm of an unconscious young woman in a pretty pink dress. She chewed with a loud smacking of lips. Her eyes looked up to see the source of this unwanted interruption. Her throat gulped with a hearty swallow.

Palmer aimed the gun between her eyes.

Before he could squeeze off a shot, a drunk woman staggered into the bathroom, giggling to herself with a drink in one hand, knocking into him. Her giggle immediately transformed into a huge scream when she witnessed the bloody scene on the floor. The bathroom erupted into chaos. The zombie prostitute dropped her food and jumped at Palmer like a cornered animal. Palmer punched her away, then became entangled with the drunk woman and they both fell to the ground, landing on the young, bloodied victim. The zombie prostitute disappeared into the bar.

Palmer jumped back to his feet. He ordered the drunk woman to stop screaming and get into the toilet stall.

"Please don't kill me!" wailed the woman.

"Get in the stall and lock the door!" yelled Palmer, pointing the gun at her for emphasis.

She did as told, shaking uncontrollably.

Once she had locked herself in the stall, Palmer took care of the zombie victim in the pink dress, shooting her once in the temple. Inside the stall, the drunk woman shrieked at the gunshot. Fortunately, the bathroom noise didn't travel far, overwhelmed by the blasting rock and roll.

Palmer shut off the bathroom light and hurried back into the bar. He pushed through the crowd of oblivious young people yelling their conversations to be heard. He searched for the zombie prostitute but couldn't find her. After a thorough search of the tavern, he concluded she had left, stumbling back into the streets of Pittsburgh.

Palmer exited the bar. He wandered up and down the block for several minutes, then heard the first siren. He knew that Harvey's Tavern had officially become a crime scene and it was time to leave the neighborhood.

As Palmer drove off in the van, he saw the patrons of Harvey's Tavern spill out onto the sidewalk, horrified and confused. Palmer continued to drive around the city, searching for the zombie prostitute, praying that she was the only remaining carrier of the virus—outside of Chaz Singleton. Deep inside, he knew it was a hopeless wish.

Palmer's worst fears were confirmed by the police radio that crackled with near hysteria throughout the evening. Others had been bitten. And now they were doing the biting. Police were breaking up "biting attacks" all over town.

The police radio announced: "We have yet another incident...more biting attacks...this time coming from Monroeville Mall. Police presence is requested immediately. Repeat: Monroeville Mall."

**

The zombie prostitute hobbled in slow, off-balanced steps through a long alley of broken glass and dim light, still hungry.

A chubby, bespectacled man in a business suit had been following her and finally called out:

"Hey sweetie."

She stopped. She turned.

"Hey sweetie, been a while," he said. He approached her with folded money in his hand. "Fifty bucks. What do you say?"

She stared at him, uncomprehending.

He grew impatient. "You know, you know. Please, baby... We can do it right here. You know what I'm saying? Don't act like you don't know me."

She tilted her head, eyes foggy.

The chubby man leaned against a brick wall, hidden from

street view. He dropped his pants. He exposed himself.

"Let's have those soft lips, baby," he said. "Wet my whistle."

She stared at the erection. She stepped over to him, intrigued by the offering. She kneeled before him.

He smiled. "That's it. Do your magic, baby."

She began to deliver on his expectations, and he moaned in pleasure. Then, quite rapidly, the encounter became something else entirely.

She dined with a ravished hunger and his screams could be heard from blocks away.

CHAPTER 22

Chaz emerged from the Holland Tunnel and plunged into New York City, immediately snared in a mad crisscross of traffic, pedestrians and towering buildings under a half-hidden gray sky. Car horns blasted regularly, as if conversing in their own special language. Cabs packed the lanes and jumped and stopped in fits to gain ground on other vehicles and each other. Jaywalkers stepped across the roads with tough, determined stares, as if daring a confrontation. This tight, concrete jungle was a long way from the tranquil sprawl of his Arizona desert, replacing an open deference to nature with a tense congestion of man-made sights and sounds.

Chaz headed north, making slow progress past Soho, Greenwich Village and, eventually, Midtown. The tourist trap of Times Square and Broadway brought traffic to a steamy crawl. When he finally made it to the Upper West Side, he was more than happy to check off the first item on his list:

Ditch the car.

Chaz parked next to a fire hydrant on 86th Street, pulled his travel bag out of the backseat and said farewell to his loyal transportation vehicle. He sent a silent thanks to Frank Olsen for providing a means of achieving his final goal: to see his son, Peter.

Chaz began the long walk up Columbus Drive. He knew he looked like hell, everything from his sickly blue skin to the bullet holes in his clothing, but among the preoccupied, seen-it-all New Yorkers, no one appeared to notice or take interest.

When he made it to Peter's Columbia University dormitory, he gently extracted a sealed white envelope with his son's name on it from his travel bag. He gave it to the security man in the lobby and said, "Please see that he gets this. It's very important."

The frumpy man at the desk muttered something and took it.

Chaz left the dorm and headed to Central Park.

He tried to imagine his son's reaction when he read the note, which began with Peter's childhood nickname, known only to the immediate family.

Rascal,

It's me. I know it's hard to believe. I don't believe it myself, but it's true. The funeral was a fake. I've been away. I will explain everything.

Meet me in Central Park by the bridge near Delacorte Theatre. I will be waiting for you.

Please don't share this note or my reappearance with anyone. Dangerous forces are after me. You will soon find out why.

Seeing you again is the most important thing in my life. I have traveled thousands of miles and literally returned from the dead for this moment.

I love you, son.

Dad

At the meeting location in Central Park, Chaz found a bench and sat. He felt a soothing calm, sheltered under expansive trees, tucked away in one of the world's busiest cities. He was finished running. He had been in motion for days—desperate to find peace ever since he escaped the massacre at the defense research bunker.

Now, in this moment, he almost felt relaxed.

He watched the pedestrians on the path in front of him. Joggers, couples holding hands, parents with infants in strollers, dog walkers. The natural flow of life returned him to simpler times, before he had the weight of the world on his shoulders.

Hours passed, but Chaz wasn't counting them. He would sit at that bench as long as it took.

Occasionally he glimpsed an approaching young man who

sparked excitement but turned out to be someone else. The pangs of disappointment gave way to more hope.

Then, as the afternoon sun began to set, a young man in blue jeans and a purple hoodie sweatshirt appeared, walking slow, eyes searching, expression uncertain, the white note in his grasp.

"Peter."

Chaz stood.

Peter stopped on the path. He stared at the man calling his name. His eyes couldn't make the connection at first—Chaz's appearance had certainly altered and his very presence was wholly improbable. Yet, there he stood, facing his son.

"Dad?"

"Yes, it's really me."

"But...how?" Peter walked closer to his father and studied him.

"I know," said Chaz with a shrug. "It's…crazy."

Peter rushed forward and threw his arms around Chaz in an embrace. Chaz held him tight.

"Dad, you're alive. Oh my God, you're alive."

"Everything is backwards," said Chaz in a soft voice, and he realized he would have to break the news that while he was alive, Peter's mother had died. Very soon, the Tucson medical examiner would identify the third victim of the townhouse fire and throw Peter's world into a brand new upheaval.

Chaz couldn't bring himself to tell Peter about his mother at this moment. Her infidelity and the staged construction "accident" would also have to wait. He needed to start with his current state of affairs.

"Dad," said Peter, when they finally broke off the embrace. "No offense, but you really smell."

"I can explain," Chaz responded, and he began his story. He revealed the secrets of Operation Invincible. Peter listened, not believing at first, then realizing he had no choice.

Chaz told Peter about the classified military experiment, the reanimation of human life and the failed attempt to build a new breed of soldier. He told him about the destruction of the medical lab and the ruthless mission to wipe out any evidence of its existence. He explained the difference between the dumb zombies and the breakthrough "smart" zombie treatment that preserved free will and intelligence. Finally, to top it all off, Chaz broke the news on the dietary issue.

"No way," said Peter.

"How could I even make up something like that?"

"I don't know," admitted Peter. "You were never big on imagination. That was more my bag."

"So this brings me to my request...and this is the hardest thing of all," said Chaz. "But it's the only place to go from here."

"What is it?" asked Peter.

"I came to New York to do what I never had a chance to do before: say goodbye."

"Goodbye?"

"Peter, I died. And I belong dead...not like this. I'm sick and not getting better. I'm infected with this disease and I'm putting everyone else at risk. I came to New York to tell you how much I love you, how proud I am of you, and to create some closure. There are people out there who want me destroyed, and I can't blame them. I pose a risk to society. I need to go down, but I don't want some slimy government assassin to do it. Peter, I have a gun. I want you to do the honors. You'll need to shoot me in the head. We'll say our goodbyes and then..."

"No!" said Peter. "Absolutely not. I'm not going to shoot my father."

"It's the only logical way to end this madness," said Chaz.

"Out of the question. You come all the way out here to tell me you're not dead and that I should kill you? Do you know how messed up that is?"

"I can't go on like this."

"Dad..." said Peter, shaking his head, and Chaz could tell his son had reached his limit. "Don't make me do this. You can't."

At that moment, Chaz saw something rustling in nearby bushes. He could discern a shadow moving behind the greenery, someone deliberately hiding...and spying.

"Get down!" shouted Chaz to Peter, and he pulled out his gun, aiming into the bushes. "Come out with your hands up! I swear to God, I'll shoot."

After a tense couple of seconds, a young woman with pale

cheeks emerged from behind the shrubs, shrouded in black. Dyed black hair cascaded down to the shoulders of a black leather jacket. She wore black eyeliner and a nose ring. She put her hands up in the air and exclaimed, "It's cool, it's cool, I'm..."

Peter finished for her. "She's my girlfriend, Dad. Dad, meet Rachel."

Chaz stared at her, stunned. He lowered the gun. "You've been watching and listening this whole time?"

"Dad," said Peter, "when I got your note I freaked out. I didn't know if it was a joke or some weird ploy to lure me into a trap. Ever since I did that documentary on street gangs, I've pissed off some people. What did you expect me to think? 'Dad's in town, he's risen from the grave and would like to have lunch.' Get real. Rachel came with to back me up and call the police in case of any funny business."

"I'm just here to protect him," said Rachel. "Honest."

"Did you call the police?" asked Chaz.

"No. But I heard everything."

"Great," muttered Chaz.

"Mr. Singleton, I know this isn't what you want to hear," said Rachel, coming over closer to both of them. "But I am totally into the Goth scene, and if it's true that you're, well, a zombie... That is probably the coolest thing I've ever heard in my life."

"It's not cool," said Chaz with a sad sigh.

"I live for the dead," said Rachel. "Music, books, fashion, you name it. I'm totally into the dark arts."

"It's true," said Peter. "She loves all that stuff and, you should also know, I love her."

"Congratulations," said Chaz.

"Can I touch you?" asked Rachel. "I've never touched a real zombie before."

"Be my guest."

Rachel came over and took Chaz's hand in her own. Her fingernails were painted black. "Oh, you're cold," she said, not repulsed but impressed.

Chaz withdrew his hand.

"For what it's worth," said Rachel, "I agree with Peter. He shouldn't shoot you. You're like a miracle. You could be a celebrity. You could go on the talk shows and get your own reality series. You could be a God to the Goth scene."

"Not interested," said Chaz. "I just want this nightmare to end."

"Dad, science got you this far, saving your life, maybe they could find a way to cure your disease or curb your appetite."

"Don't be so bummed," said Rachel. "You get to be a zombie. I'm jealous."

"Dad, you need a place to stay," said Peter. "You could stay with me in the dorm, at least for a little while."

"No. It's not safe," said Chaz. "The people who are after me—they would find me there. In fact, it's probably not safe for you, either, right now. They might come after you to get to me. I never should have gotten you involved."

"I've got an idea," said Rachel. "Why don't you both stay at my apartment? I'm in Harlem. Nobody will come after you there."

Chaz started to shake his head, but Peter responded, "Yes. Great idea. Dad, let's do it. The three of us can stay there and plan your next move."

"Where else would you go?" asked Rachel.

Chaz shrugged. He relented. "Alright. Just for a few days."

"Let's get a cab to the dorm," said Peter. "I'll pack some stuff and then we'll go to Rachel's pad."

Chaz looked at Rachel. "Are you sure you want to harbor a zombie fugitive?"

"I would be honored," she replied.

**

The three of them left Central Park and flagged a yellow cab. The driver took them to Peter's dormitory. Chaz and Rachel waited in the backseat while Peter ran in to gather his belongings.

"While I'm at your apartment, we have to keep it a secret," Chaz told Rachel. "You can't tell your Goth friends. You can't have people over. I need to stay hidden. It's important for your safety and the safety of my son."

"Understood," said Rachel. "I won't tell a soul. Cross my heart and hope to die." Then she giggled.

**

In a white van parked across the street from the dorm, Breck Palmer sat with a .357 Magnum.

For a split second, he had a perfect shot at Chaz's skull, but then the young woman in black shifted in her seat, blocking him. The steady flow of pedestrians and traffic also posed a problem, not to mention the ample police presence. This was simply a lousy place to attempt a shot.

No worries. Palmer had made it this far, armed with Chaz's address book, fully anticipating that the smart zombie would come here to see his son. It was another failing of the "smart zombie" concept... Sentimentality. Emotional attachment. Commitment to family.

Such traits never would have worked for a new breed of super soldiers who must fight the enemy without conscience or personal baggage.

The son returned to the cab with a backpack and bulging duffel bag. The cabbie popped the trunk and the son tossed in his belongings. He returned to the backseat to join his father and the girl.

All three of them had to die. Chaz, of course, the priority, but now he had added two witnesses and accomplices, whom no doubt had learned about Operation Invincible.

Three murders in New York City would not create too much of a stink.

The yellow cab advanced forward, joining the traffic north into Harlem.

Breck Palmer started up the van and followed, the gun resting alongside him in the passenger seat.

CHAPTER 23

Evening fell on New York City, prompting headlights and streetlamps. The yellow cab dropped off its passengers in a troubled section of Harlem overrun by graffiti scrawl, boarded up storefronts, abandoned shells of cars and slow, wandering souls with no place to go: no job, no home, no money and blank stares. At first glance, they appeared to be zombies. Closer inspection still suggested zombies—just not the back-from-the-dead, flesh-eating type.

Peter, recognizing his father's concern, told him, "It's okay, Dad. That's why the rent here is so cheap."

They pulled Peter's belongings out of the trunk. After getting paid, the cabbie anxiously peeled out of the neighborhood, blasting his horn at a group of scrawny teenagers dashing across the street in reversed baseball caps and low-hanging trousers.

"Hi, Phil," said Rachel to an elderly man with tattered clothing and a face full of scars.

Leaning against a brick wall for support, Phil gestured with a boney arm. "Spare a cig?"

She gave him a cigarette and he grinned with sporadic, Halloween pumpkin teeth. "Thank you, thank you."

Rachel, Chaz and Peter entered a tall, colorless apartment building, stepping across assorted debris.

"Sorry for the urine smell," said Rachel. "Some of the street people use the front lobby for a toilet."

"I can't smell anything," said Chaz. But he could hear—and as they climbed the stairwell, the inside of the building came alive with sounds permeating thin walls: coarse television voices, crying babies, barking dogs.

On the fourth floor, Rachel led them down a skinny corridor to her door and unlocked it with a heavy CHUNK!

As they entered, Chaz was relieved to see her place was clean and tidy, although definitely decorated in her own oddball style.

Continuing the Gothic theme, the apartment was draped in a lot of black. She also favored wrought iron furnishings and candles. A large raven statue dominated a table on one side of the room. "That's Poe," said Rachel.

Posters on the wall celebrated various icons of the darker side of pop culture—Marilyn Manson, Rob Zombie, Diamanda Galas. A shelving unit bulged with books and DVDs continuing the obsession with the macabre. Chaz complimented Rachel on her extensive horror collection, which explained her fascination with him, a true-life, walking and talking horror movie.

Chaz wished he was in a movie instead of experiencing his horrors for real. To him, Rachel was no different than the kids from his youth who grew up entertained by war movies without ever experiencing the ugly brutality of real combat.

Peter plopped his overnight bag on the far end of a long, black leather sofa. "Anybody up for a glass of red wine?" he asked. "I know I am."

"Great idea," said Rachel. "I have a bottle of—"

And she never finished her sentence because that's when the gunfire began.

A rapid, relentless pounding of bullets burst the living room window and began tearing up the apartment. Chaz felt a bullet strike his head and thought for sure he was a goner. He screamed, "Get down!" and dove to the shag rug. He put a hand into his hair, felt wetness and discovered the bullet had missed his skull by centimeters—and pretty much decimated his left ear.

The steady onslaught continued, bullets biting into the furniture and walls. Chaz realized the curtain-free windows and descent of nightfall left them exposed like a fish bowl. The bullet that destroyed his ear had no doubt been aimed for his brain.

"Stay down!" shouted Chaz. Spread out on his back, he yanked his own gun out of its holster. He aimed for the ceiling— the large, circular lamp that lit up the living room.

Chaz fired, exploding the bulb into a rain of shards, plunging the room into darkness.

After a moment of silence, a fresh barrage of bullets sprayed the apartment. The attacker was well stocked. Chaz glanced across the room and saw Peter and Rachel petrified, hugging the floor.

"Listen, there's a sniper after me," said Chaz. "How do I get to the roof?"

"At the top of the stairs, there's a ladder," said Rachel. "It should be open, New York fire regulations. I—I go up there all the time to smoke."

"Good." Chaz jumped to his feet. At that moment, the sniper must have seen movement in the shadows because the gunfire accelerated.

Chaz heard Rachel scream. Bullets shattered a mirror, punctured the leather sofa and tore feathers off of Poe.

Chaz slipped out the apartment door. He raced down the corridor, where several neighbors congregated.

"Damn those gangbangers," muttered an old woman, weary, as if a rain of bullets was a common weather pattern to wait out.

Chaz hustled up the stairs, determined to stop this sniper, regretting that now his son and his son's girlfriend were involved—and endangered.

Chaz's mission was clear: kill or be killed.

He climbed the ladder and popped the top that allowed him on the roof. Once on the roof, he crouched low, moving from vent to chimney to antennae, staying concealed as much as possible as he made his way to the edge. The lights of New York City sparkled around him and a cool breeze blew across the rooftop.

Chaz finally spotted his attacker.

Breck Palmer stood on a fire escape on the building across the street from Rachel's apartment. Partly hidden from view by a clothesline of drying laundry, he wore dark assassin colors. He held a rifle with a powerful scope in his hands; boxes of ammunition were at his feet.

Chaz knew he did not have many bullets left in his own gun. The handgun also would not be as easy to stabilize as a rifle. Palmer didn't see Chaz yet, his eyes affixed on Rachel's apartment, but that could change at any minute.

Chaz needed a precise hit. He didn't have a lot of cover on

the rooftop. If Palmer squeezed off an accurate shot and stopped Chaz's zombie brain, Peter and Rachel would be next. Palmer would not allow them to live with the knowledge they now possessed. They would be slaughtered just like Dr. Rabe and the rest of the Operation Invincible medical staff.

Palmer fired a new round into Rachel's apartment, revealing his exact location in the dark through the flashes of light accompanying the spray of bullets.

Chaz aimed, said a silent prayer, and squeezed off a shot.

Instead of the desired *ooph*, he heard a *ping* as the bullet hit off the fire escape, very close to Palmer, but missing the intended target.

Palmer stopped firing into Rachel's apartment. Chaz could see his shadow move behind a long, flapping, white bed sheet. The barrel of the rifle emerged from between the sheet and a hanging bath towel. The rifle pointed up at the rooftop.

Chaz aimed his gun. "*You're* the monster," he said through clenched teeth.

The rifle spat a round of bullets on and around Chaz. He felt several strike his chest but refused to lose his balance, aiming with razor-sharp focus at the dark shape behind the white sheet.

Chaz fired.

A spray of red splashed across the bed sheet.

Chaz saw Breck Palmer drop his rifle, spinning from the impact, getting caught up in the laundry on the clothesline.

Entangled in towels and sheets, Breck Palmer toppled over the edge of the fire escape. His body fell fast out of view. Chaz heard an ugly thud as it struck the concrete below.

"Your turn in Hell," muttered Chaz. He straightened up and took one last look at the empty fire escape. The laundry on the clothesline waved in the wind.

Chaz placed the gun back in its holster and left the roof's edge to return inside the building.

Chaz stepped back into Rachel's apartment, greeted by an eerie silence. Even in the dark, he could tell that the place had been shredded by gunfire.

"It's over," announced Chaz. "At least for now."

He heard whimpering and froze.

"Peter?" he said.

"Dad, over here."

Chaz hurried toward the voice. He found Peter in the bathroom, lying on the floor with Rachel, bloodied, in his arms.

"Dad, she's been hit."

"Shit," said Chaz, and he knelt down. He could tell right away that it was bad.

"I can't stop the bleeding," said Peter, tears in his eyes.

Rachel struggled to stay alert, eyes thinning.

"Don't let me die," she said, slurred.

"Where's she hit?" asked Chaz.

"I'm not sure. All over. Dad, we can't let her die."

"Make me one of you," said Rachel.

"What?" said Chaz.

"Come closer..." she murmured.

"We'll get help," said Chaz.

"Please," she gasped, and then she said something else but her words grew faint.

Chaz leaned closer.

Rachel abruptly sat up. She stuck out her pierced tongue and licked the side of Chaz's face, where part of his ear had been shot off.

She sucked on the blood like a hungry vampire, using all of her remaining strength.

Chaz pulled back, shoving her away, alarmed. "What the hell are you doing?"

Rachel answered. "Becoming...one of you."

Her eyes closed.

Within seconds, she went limp.

Peter cried, seated in his girlfriend's blood, still holding her in his arms.

Chaz checked for a pulse in her neck and found none. He stood up, shaken. "She licked my blood, Peter."

"Dad..." said Peter. "She was delirious."

"No, you don't understand. I'm infected. She... She's going to come back."

Peter stared up at his father. "Like one of you?"

"No, like one of the...others. It won't be her anymore. She'll

126

just be this walking bag of impulses. She won't even know you. She won't be able to talk or think. Her only instinct will be to feed on the living...and spread the virus."

"But Dad, it will bring her back."

"It's not what you think," said Chaz.

"She will have eternal life."

"I can't allow this to happen," said Chaz. "I know you're going to hate me, but I really have no choice." He took out his gun. He aimed it at Rachel's forehead. "Move away from her, Peter."

"Dad, no!" Peter lunged at his father. Chaz grabbed him with his free arm. He shoved his son out of the bathroom with such force that Peter stumbled backwards and fell to the floor.

Chaz aimed the gun between Rachel's eyes and squeezed the trigger.

Click.

Chaz sighed. He lowered the gun. "Out of bullets."

Peter sat on the floor outside the bathroom. He still had tears in his eyes. "Okay, Dad... Now what?"

"We need ammunition." Chaz turned to face his son.

"Dad..."

"Not just for her. For protecting ourselves. I may have stopped that sniper, but there will be others. I'm a government secret let loose in the public. You're an accomplice. I never should have dragged you into this. It would have been better for you to continue believing I was dead. I don't know why I did this. I guess I wanted closure. It was selfish."

"No, Dad," said Peter, standing back up. "The fact that you came all this way...went through everything that you did to get here...it means the world to me."

Chaz just looked at his son, saddened.

"I'm going to stick by you, Dad," said Peter. "I won't let them get you. We'll protect one another. I'll get a gun, too."

"Peter..."

"Seriously. I'm not going to go through another attack like that unarmed."

"Where are we going to get guns and ammo?"

"I have a contact."

"A contact for guns and ammo?"

"Yes, sort of." Peter explained, "My documentary for school. The one that won first place. It was about the gang scene in New York. I interviewed gang members. A lot of them. I know people who could help us...in an emergency, which this is."

"Guns from gang members?"

"For the right price, no questions asked. Yes."

Chaz gave it serious thought. He didn't like weaving his son into this dangerous adventure any further, but there really wasn't an alternative.

"Alright," said Chaz. "I have money. Let's see what your contacts can do for us. We have to act fast. We can't stay here much longer."

"I'll make some calls right now," said Peter, and he pulled out his cell phone.

"Wait," said Chaz. His eyes returned to the bloodied body of Rachel on the bathroom floor. Her lips remained red with Chaz's blood. "We can't leave her like this."

"Where do we take her?" asked Peter, glancing at her, then quickly away, overwhelmed by the painful image of his girlfriend's fate.

"We don't take her anywhere," said Chaz. "We need to make sure she stays here."

Peter grew puzzled. "What do you mean? It's not like she can just get up and walk away..."

Chaz gave him a long look.

Peter nodded. "Oh. Right. She *can* do that."

"Is there anything here we can use to tie her up and keep her from getting out of the apartment? There's no telling when she might wake up with an appetite. We can't risk it. Is there any rope around here?"

"Rope? No." Peter thought for a moment. "How about handcuffs?"

"Handcuffs?"

"I'll go get them," said Peter. "They're in the bedroom."

"Bedroom?" said Chaz.

"She liked to play...games," said Peter, and he blushed.

Chaz didn't press it any further. "Just get them. Quick."

They handcuffed one of Rachel's wrists to the pipe under the sink. Chaz gave it several hard tugs. Secure.

Peter placed the key in his pocket.

They looked at the limp, lifeless, bloodied Rachel one more time. Then Chaz gently closed the bathroom door.

"You okay?" said Chaz to Peter, who still appeared pale and badly shaken up.

"Am I okay?" Peter responded. Sarcasm overtook his tone. "Of course I'm okay. My dad has gone from dead to alive, and my girlfriend has gone from alive to dead, but other than that, I am just dandy."

"That reminds me," said Chaz with a heavy sigh. "I'm afraid I have some rather bad news about your mother..."

CHAPTER 24

Early the next morning, Chaz and Peter took the subway to Hunts Point, a neighborhood in South Bronx frequented by shootings and stabbings in an endless cycle of retaliation in the turf wars between the Assassins and the Royalz.

Chaz and Peter sat together, surrounded by a jumble of commuters, saying very little. Chaz continued to stay pragmatic, guided by his to-do list: get guns, get ammo, then search out a new hideaway. Peter, on the other hand, had become even more numb than his zombie father, emotionally drained by the past 24 hours of transitions between life and death for his closest loved ones. He had gobbled a couple of Rachel's Xanax to settle his nerves and hold off a massive panic attack.

When they arrived at their destination, Chaz noted that the train's creepiest, downtrodden passengers exited with them, and he knew he was in for a treat even more sordid than the Harlem neighborhood they had left. Prostitutes and drug sellers marketed their services from sidewalks in front of long-shuttered storefronts.

"Follow me," said Peter. "It's not far."

Peter took them to a large auto salvage lot, essentially a junk yard with an admission fee. Occasionally, brave souls paid to go searching for spare parts. A far corner of the lot also served as the makeshift headquarters for the Royalz, an ethnically mixed gang with a common denomination of hate and violence.

Peter had interviewed two of their leaders, Troy and his tubby sidekick, "Juice" for a documentary project for his Columbia University film class. Rather than being private and guarded, the gangbangers thrived on the opportunity for publicity, and opened up quite nicely to the camera, stopping just short of saying anything that could get them immediately incarcerated.

The front of the salvage yard was anchored by a long trailer. Peter banged on the front door until it opened a crack.

"I'm Peter. This is my dad. We're friends of Troy and Juice."

"Ten dollars," said a deep voice inside the door crack.

"Ten?" said Peter. "Last time it was—"

"Fifteen."

Peter got the message and shut up. He dug fifteen dollars out of his wallet and passed them through the crack, where they were suctioned away by a large hand.

"You know the way in?" said the voice.

Peter nodded.

"Thirty minutes. Then I sic the dogs on you." The door shut.

Chaz turned to Peter. "Are we going to be okay?"

"What does it matter, my life is already in danger," said Peter. "Follow me."

Peter walked over to a large, faded "Drink Coca Cola!" sign propped sideways in the dirt against a tall wire fence. He pulled it back to reveal a gaping hole in the fence.

"I'll go first, they need to see me," said Peter, and he ducked and entered. Chaz followed.

The lot held long rows of gutted vehicles, some of them literally stacked on top of one another. They stepped through a graveyard of deceased brands: Oldsmobile, Plymouth, Geo, Pontiac and Saturn. Many vehicles yawned with open hoods, revealing missing engines. Most doors were open or broken off. Some cars sat low to the ground, without tires, melded into the landscape with weeds growing through them.

Peter maneuvered through a maze of random debris: broken pallets, chunks of glass, and even an old mattress.

Chaz followed. His eyes caught a glimpse of movement up ahead. He froze. "Wait," he said to Peter.

They stood still and after a moment, a head peeked over the top of a cream-colored Buick speckled with brownish patches of rust.

Peter waved. "Juice, it's me," he called out. "It's cool."

"Movie boy!" greeted a voice behind them.

Peter and Chaz turned and Troy approached, wearing a

bandana on his head and a large basketball jersey over a black t-shirt. Juice hustled over from the Buick, fat, crew-cut and perspiring.

Peter watched their eyes gravitate towards his father.

"It's okay," said Peter. "It's my Dad."

Troy stared at Chaz. "Hell man, you sick?"

"Yes," said Chaz. "Believe me, you don't want what I got."

Troy promptly stepped back. He turned and addressed Peter, "So, movie boy, you back for another interview? I gotta get my hair done."

"No, no cameras," said Peter.

Troy appeared disappointed. Juice took a swing at a wasp.

"I need some guns," said Peter. "Handguns and ammo."

"Hell, no, you gonna get me busted."

"I swear to God, this has nothing to do with the documentary. It's just between you and me."

Troy shook his head and spat a wad of phlegm to the dirt. "Damn, movie boy."

"I've been level with you about everything else, haven't I? We're prepared to pay...pay extra."

Troy looked at the ground. "I can get you guns," he said in a low mumble. "Meet me on the bus in ten minutes."

Peter smiled. "Excellent. Thank you."

"C'mon, Juice." Troy headed down an aisle of cars with Juice trailing by several slow, waddling steps.

Chaz turned to Peter, worried. "We're going to make this deal on a bus? Won't there be witnesses?"

"No," said Peter. "Over there. *That* bus."

He pointed to a far side of the junkyard where an abandoned yellow school bus sat, missing all four tires, decorated with multicolor gang graffiti. "That's their headquarters."

"Got it," said Chaz.

After ten minutes, Peter and Chaz advanced to the school bus. They passed an old hearse with broken windows and a body in the back. "Holy—" said Chaz, and then he realized the body was alive, injecting a syringe into a forearm wrapped tight by a rubber hose.

"Heroin addict," said Peter to his father.

"And *I'm* considered the zombie," grumbled Chaz.

They stopped at the back of the school bus, where a large sheet hung over the hole where an emergency exit door once existed

"Don't stand around, get in here!" said Troy sharply from behind the sheet.

Peter and Chaz stepped up and slid inside the bus. Troy sat in one of the long green seats, about one-third back. Juice sat several rows further, silently observing and wiping sweat from his brow.

Crouched to avoid hitting their heads on the low ceiling, Peter and Chaz walked down the aisle, stepping over a makeshift crack cocaine pipe created out of a grape soda can.

"Let's do this fast," said Troy. He waved them over to his seat, which spouted stuffing from several large gashes. "Feast your eyes." He lifted a blanket, revealing the merchandise.

"This here, a nine millimeter Glock, semi-automatic, or you might want the Model 686 revolver, Smith and Wesson. Personally, I like the Beretta..."

Before Peter could say anything, Chaz stated, "We'll take it all. Plus as much ammo as you can provide right now."

As Troy handled the payment, he shouted to Juice: "Yo, get our customers a bag or somethin'."

Juice dug around the layers of trash on the bus floor and found a plastic Target bag. He handed it over and Chaz spilled the guns and bullets into it.

The four of them exited the bus, stepping back into the lot. "Now get out of here," said Troy. "I mean it. This never happened. And, movie boy, if you put this in one of your movies, I swear to God..."

Juice spoke up for the first time, finishing the sentence in a high pitch that revealed his pre-pubescence: "We'll blow your motherfucking head off!"

"Got it," said Peter.

Chaz said, "Let's get out of here." He took one step and then Troy shouted, "Shit! Nobody move!"

Everyone froze.

"I see somethin' I don't like...back by those forklifts," said

Troy.

A shot rang out. Juice grabbed his neck and hollered in pain. Blood bubbled from between his fingers.

"It's the Assassins!" screamed Troy.

A half-dozen rival gang members surfaced from various points around the junk yard, delivering a flurry of bullets. The gunfire kicked up dirt, tore holes through metal and shattered glass.

"Dad, let's get out of here!" shouted Peter. He broke into a run, fleeing from the bus. Chaz followed, keeping his eyes on the location of the attackers.

Even on Xanax, Peter could feel the adrenaline surge. He ran as fast as he could for the hole in the fence. He shouted back at his father, "They don't want us—we're just in the crossfire. We'll be safe if we get out of here."

When Peter reached the cyclone fence, he spun around and discovered his father was no longer behind him.

"Dad? Dad where are you?" he cried out.

Several car aisles away, Peter glimpsed his father running toward one of the shooters. A rival gang member had holed up inside the back of an abandoned bread truck.

"Jesus, Dad, this is no time to take sides!"

He watched as his father disappeared inside the truck. He heard more shots, then a big scream.

It wasn't his father's scream.

Peter waited for several minutes, hoping to see his father emerge, but the truck fell silent.

Peter grew agitated, then worried.

The gunfire grew concentrated around the school bus, where Troy had retreated inside. He fired back with an assault rifle from one of the broken windows. At least he hadn't sold *all* of his firearms.

"Damn it, Dad!" muttered Peter. He ducked low and scurried back through the aisles of junked cars to retrieve his father.

He made it to the rear of the bread truck without incident and cautiously climbed inside. He saw the plastic bag with the gun purchases tossed off to the side. His eyes needed to adjust to see anything in the far reaches of the cargo area.

Peter listened. He could hear a persistent smacking sound, like somebody eating a sandwich. He peered into the darkness.

"Dad...?" Peter took several paces forward and then he caught sight of something he really didn't want to see.

The Assassins gang member lay sprawled on his back, not moving, as Peter's father dined on his flesh like a large, messy pizza.

"Dad! What the hell!"

"Do you mind?" snapped Chaz.

Peter returned to the outer edge of the truck, trying desperately to erase the image that had just been burned into his brain.

He stared across the yard at the yellow school bus. He could see members of the Assassins street gang swarming the bus from all sides. The gunshots intensified, then grew sporadic, then stopped. Cheers erupted.

No doubt, Troy was history.

BANG.

A loud gunshot echoed inside the truck, causing Peter to jump.

His father emerged from the shadows, blood staining his chin like barbeque sauce. He gripped the bag of gun purchases.

"He's down for good," said Chaz, and Peter knew what that meant: a shot to the brain to prevent the chewed up carcass from rising from the dead to start up an all-new street gang: the New York Zombeez.

The gunshot chilled Peter to the bones. He knew it was the same fate that awaited Rachel.

As they returned to the train station, Chaz, energized by a full belly, tried to laugh off the ugly scene that Peter had just witnessed.

"You know how most children are embarrassed by their father? I just took it to a new level."

"Not funny, Dad," said Peter. "Not funny at all. Let's just not talk about it."

**

Chaz and Peter returned to Rachel's apartment.

Peter sat on the bullet-ridden couch and buried his face in his hands.

"I know what you have to do," he said, solemn. "Just do it and get it over with."

"I'm sorry, Peter," said Chaz. He held his new revolver. "It's for the best."

Chaz left for the bathroom.

He opened the door. Then he exclaimed, "Holy shit!"

Peter jumped up to join his father.

Together they stared into the bathroom, stunned. Rachel was gone. But not all of Rachel. Her arm remained handcuffed to the pipe beneath the sink, severed near the elbow.

"What the hell?" said Peter.

"She got away," muttered Chaz. "She chewed off her own arm to escape."

"Oh my God."

"We gotta find her before it's too late." Chaz spun around and headed for the door. "Come on! There's no telling what damage she could do let loose out there." He ordered his son: "Grab the other gun."

They ran out of the apartment, dashed down the staircase and spilled into the street.

Stopping for a moment, they examined every direction.

"Which way do you think she went?" asked Peter.

"I have no idea," said Chaz. "Damn it! We have to find her."

"If you had to guess, which direction would she take? You're a zombie, you should know."

"She would go in the direction of the most people," responded Chaz. "She would go where the food is."

They advanced down the sidewalk, loaded guns tucked under their shirts, toward a busy intersection populated with stores and restaurants.

"Over there!" cried out Peter.

A small crowd gathered outside an electronics store. Expecting to find their escapee, Peter and Chaz ran up to the layers of shocked faces—but Rachel was not the center of their attention.

They were staring at the store's display window, where a widescreen, hi-definition television ("On Sale Now!") broadcast an alarming story on one of the national news networks.

"Is this real or some kinda horror movie?" asked a young man with a backpack.

"It's really happening, it's all over the news," responded an older African American woman carrying shopping bags.

Chaz couldn't hear the television audio through the storefront glass, but the images told him all he needed to know. A frightened reporter spoke on camera from outside a shopping mall, surrounded by police cars and ambulances, with the words "PITTSBURGH CANNIBALISM ATTACKS" in big, bold letters at the foot of the screen.

Voices from the crowd swirled in Chaz's ears.

"It's happening all over Pittsburgh."

"Some kind of biting disease."

"Must be a terrorist attack!"

"They took them to the hospital and now the whole hospital is quarantined."

"I heard 20 dead."

"No, it's double that now."

Chaz slowly stepped back from the crowd. He stopped at the curb and hung his head, overwhelmed with grief and hopelessness.

"Dad..." Peter joined him. "Dad, it's not your fault."

Chaz looked up at his son. "I'm sorry, Peter. But yes it is."

CHAPTER 25

To the people of Manhattan's upper west side, the dazed woman in black lace with the pale pallor was just one of those Goth kids emulating death. It never would have dawned on them that this was the real thing hobbling down the sidewalk on a sunny Saturday morning.

If they gave her a second or third glance, they might have noticed that a hand failed to emerge from her left leather sleeve but written it off to a fashion statement. They also may have seen the splotches of red around her mouth but figured it was a deliberate and defiantly sloppy application of lipstick.

She crossed streets with little regard for cars, like so many preoccupied New Yorkers, eyes fixed ahead with unflappable determination.

She felt nothing and thought about even less, just two pudgy legs in torn black tights carrying her around with the instinct of a wind-up toy. When a stirring sensation emerged from the nothingness, it triggered curiosity, then a slow, gradual identification.

Hunger.

The stoic, brisk pedestrians around her transformed into food. She swiveled her head in various directions, experiencing a deep grumbling in her belly at the sight of human flesh.

A large, beefy man in a short-sleeve New York Yankees jersey stood with a companion at a bus stop. His stationary stance offered an irresistible temptation for a dine and dash.

She approached him.

"What the hell, bitch!"

The large man in the Yankees jersey yanked his arm away, but it was too late. She had punctured the skin with bite marks and a tantalizing taste of his living tissue.

The man's friend gave her a forceful shove and exclaimed,

"Get away from us, you freak!" She stumbled back several steps, saying nothing. The two men stared in astonishment at the bite mark.

"She bit you?"

"Yeah, can you believe it? What a nut job."

"You better get that checked out."

"I'm okay."

"No, really. She could have some disease."

"I paid two hundred bucks for these box seats, I'm not gonna miss the game. Get real, Herve, they're playing the Red Sox!"

"She's probably got rabies," joked the friend.

"I'll get it checked after the game. It's just a cut. Crazy bitch."

Then the bus arrived and took them away to Yankee Stadium.

Rachel continued her journey down the sidewalk, still relishing the nip of hairy forearm, a small hors d'oeuvres before the main feast to come.

**

Breck Palmer awoke in terrible pain: broken legs, a concussion, and a sharp ache in his left shoulder where the bullet struck bone.

The hospital room was small but isolated. An I.V. drip entered his inner elbow. A neck brace held his head in place with a firm pinch of pressure.

Everything hurt.

But far worse than the pain was the immediate smack of remembrance that Chaz Singleton had escaped, once again, to create unknown calamity upon the human race.

"Dear God," murmured Palmer.

"You're awake," said a voice.

Startled, Palmer tried to turn his head to the source of the voice—but couldn't, trapped by the neck brace, I.V. and assorted plaster casts.

"Don't move," said the voice, low and smooth. "You're seriously injured. You're lucky to be alive."

Palmer guessed a Caucasian male in his fifties or sixties. "Who..." said Palmer.

"I am Mr. G," said the voice. "I represent your interests at the highest level of national security. Up until now, we were hoping you could contain your little problem with the resources we provided. Unfortunately, we have a situation developing in Pennsylvania. The problem has grown exponentially. We are handling it as quickly as possible. A special forces unit is taking charge with top priority given to stopping the public panic. We have citizen unrest and the media are making it worse. There's a lot of work ahead. That includes finding your one-man human plague and putting him down for good."

"Where is he?" asked Palmer, each syllable a painful utterance.

"We don't know. He appears to have left the apartment in Harlem with his son and relocated. It's a big city, but we'll find him. We can't allow the infection to spread any further. If we have an outbreak in New York City, we'll have a global catastrophe on our hands."

Mr. G's footsteps left the bedside and his voice trailed as he departed through the door. "Your damage is done, Breck Palmer. Welcome to your legacy."

Palmer shut his eyes. He wanted to weep.

"Hey there, sunshine!" chirped a happy female voice minutes later. A nurse stepped into his view. "How are you feeling? I know, it can't be good. But you will get better. The worst is over. We've got you stabilized. You want to watch some television? Here, I'll sit you up so you can see the TV. Don't turn your head."

She pressed a button and the bed hummed as it elevated him into a sitting-up position.

She stepped over to a television hanging from the ceiling and turned it on. She flipped through a few channels until she found a baseball game.

"Hey," she said. "The Yankees are playing the Red Sox. That should be fun. Watch, relax, take your mind off everything else. You good?"

He couldn't even nod in the neck brace. His head was locked forward. He simply smiled, weak and crooked.

"Good," she said. She reached upward and increased the volume. The chatter of the Yankees broadcasters filled Palmer's ears.

"Be back later," said the nurse, relentlessly cheerful. She left the room and closed the door.

Staring ahead, Palmer watched the Yankees game. He really had no choice.

"It's a beautiful day at Yankee Stadium and we have a packed house," said the announcer.

A batter for the Red Sox popped out.

The next one walked, then stole second.

Then the cameras became distracted by something in the crowd. The television showed a ripple of commotion across several rows of seats.

"We have some kind of disturbance in the stands," spoke up the announcer. "Oh my. A lot of people are involved. We might have a brawl on our hands. This is crazy. It looks like they're biting one another. Is that what I'm seeing? Security is moving in. Now what... There's also fighting in the stands along the third base line. What in God's name is happening here? Now the players have stopped to watch. The umpires have called time. Oh my God, somebody just fell out of the upper deck. There's yet another commotion. I see at least three—now four—outbreaks of fighting. Look at that, they're actually biting one another. In all my years, I've never seen anything like it. Holy cow, this is unbelievable!"

Palmer wanted to turn away but he couldn't, and the chaos exploded across the big screen in front of him.

**

After walking a steady pace for countless blocks, Rachel stopped and firmly planted her feet.

This felt like a destination.

She stared, wide eyed and open mouthed, at the awesome swirl of lights, colors, noise, traffic, skyscrapers and people.

She basked in the glow of Times Square, an epicenter of tourists, locals, walkers, gawkers, talkers, old, young, big, small, all colors and tastes of the rainbow.

Stomach gurgling and teeth bared, she advanced.

Rachel had reached the ultimate buffet and she was famished.

CHAPTER 26

"You ready, Dad?"

"I think so."

"You sure?"

"Yeah. We need to do this. Let's roll."

Chaz and Peter stood in the far reaches of the auto salvage yard, their new temporary home, standing outside an old, white delivery van that held their meager belongings, always packed and ready to go on a moment's notice.

So far, no one had bothered them here. So far.

Peter had set up a simple camcorder on a tripod, pointed at his father. With a wave of his hand, he signaled they were recording. He looked into the view finder where Chaz filled the frame, head and shoulders against the generic backdrop of the side of the van.

"Hello," Chaz addressed the camera. "My name is Chaz Singleton. I died in a construction accident in Tucson, Arizona, on April 2 of this year. Without the consent or knowledge of me or my family, my body was transported to a secret biomedical research facility operated by the United States Department of Defense. I became the subject of an experiment to reanimate the dead..."

In plain language and emotionless candor, Chaz revealed everything he knew, every horrible twist and turn of his journey. He named Breck Palmer. He cited the murder of the lab's research staff and the intentional destruction of the facility. He confessed to his moments of weakness in Pittsburgh. He revealed the source of the virus currently spreading across New York City.

"This will get worse before it gets better," said Chaz. "We now have two human races. We will either live together or wipe each other out."

Chaz took full accountability and asked for no forgiveness.

"I can't undo the past. None of us can. We must accept the new reality. The future is in our hands. God help us all."

Chaz lowered his head and cried a single, black tear.

Peter used his laptop to upload the video to the Internet. Under his father's instructions, he titled it: "How I Started the Apocalypse."

EPILOGUE

Staring into her laptop screen, Dolores Lee Haggerty watched the video for the seventeenth time and then hit replay once more.

As Chaz Singleton's video confession exploded worldwide across the Internet, no one felt a deeper sense of empathy than Dolores. The video shocked, chilled and comforted her. She could relate to Chaz in ways no one else could.

Dolores was a fully cognizant corpse.

Dr. Rabe had given Dolores the same "smart zombie" brain stimulant as Chaz. Rabe had chosen her for the serum because he was smitten with her. A widower, Rabe found himself drawn to Dolores, a young beauty who died in her prime, the victim of an allergic reaction to food cooked in oil tainted with shellfish.

The night before the shutdown of the lab, Rabe had sensed potential trouble and smuggled her into his home, setting up a hidden living quarters in his basement, complete with a freezer filled with the tasty "lasagna" that she ultimately discovered was something else.

When he didn't return that fateful night, she grew afraid. When she heard about the lab explosion the next day on the news, she could immediately deduce the ugly truth behind the alleged "accident." She quickly fled Rabe's house.

She stuffed coolers with the stock of zombie meals, stole the jeep from his garage and took off for the West Coast, relocating to Portland, Oregon.

In Portland, she sold the jeep for cash and used the money to rent a cheap apartment and lay low. She lived on the dwindling supply of pre-packaged human flesh, uncertain of her course of action when the food ran out.

Rabe had never mentioned Chaz Singleton to her and now it was apparent that Chaz had never heard about her existence either.

She knew one thing for certain: as the only two of their kind, they were destined to be together.

She didn't know Chaz's whereabouts, except that he was somewhere in New York City, a population of eight million.

At least that was a start.

THE END

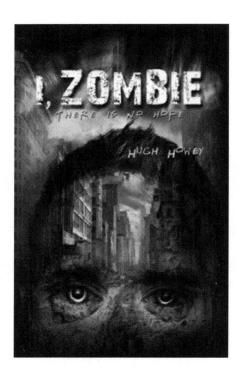

WARNING: NOT FIT FOR HUMAN CONSUMPTION

This book contains foul language and fouler descriptions of life as a zombie. It will offend most anyone, so proceed with caution or not at all.

And be forewarned: This is not a zombie book. This is a different sort of tale. It is a story about the unfortunate, about those who did not get away. It is a human story at its rotten heart. It is the reason we can't stop obsessing about these creatures, in whom we see all too much of ourselves.

Available at Amazon and all good book stores

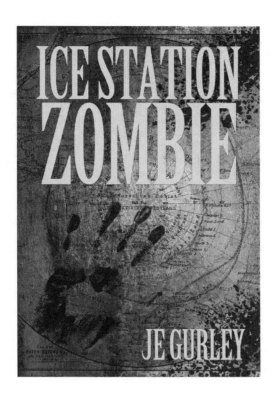

ICE STATION ZOMBIE
JE GURLEY

For most of the long, cold winter, Antarctica is a frozen wasteland. Now, the ice is melting and the zombies are thawing. Arctic explorers Val Marino and Elliot Anson race against time and death to reach Australia, but the Demise has preceded them and zombies stalk the streets of Adelaide and Coober Pedy.

www.severedpress.com

The Coalition

When the dead rose to destroy the living, Ron Cutter learned to survive. While so many others died, he thrived. His life is a constant battle against the living dead. As he casts his own bullets and packs his shotgun shells, his humanity slowly melts away.

Then he encounters a lost boy and a woman searching for a place of refuge. Can they help him recover the emotions he set aside to live? And if he does recover them, will those feelings be an asset in his struggles, or a danger to him?

THE STATE OF EXTINCTION: the first installment in the **COALITON OF THE LIVING** trilogy of Mankind's battle against the plague of the Living Dead. As recounted by author **Robert Mathis Kurtz.**

RANCID

Nothing ever happens in the middle of nowhere or in Virginia for that matter. This is why Noel and her friends found themselves on cloud nine when one of their favorite hardcore bands happened to be playing a show in their small hometown. Between the meteor shower and the short trip to the cemetery outside of town after the show, this crazy group of friends instantly plummet from those clouds into a frenzied nightmare of putrefied horror.

Is this sudden nightmare related to the showering meteors or does this small town hold even darker secrets than the rotting corpses that are surfacing?

"Zombies in small town America, a corporate conspiracy, fast paced action and a satisfying body count- what's not to like? Just don't get too attached to any character; they may die or turn zombie soon enough!" - Mainak Dhar, bestselling author of Alice in Deadland and Zombiestan

www.severedpress.com

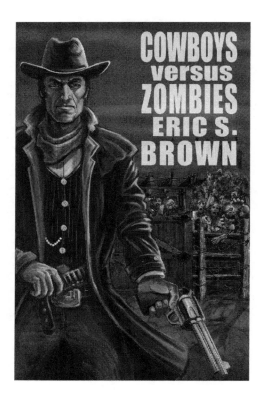

COWBOYS VS ZOMBIES

Dilouie is a killer. He's always made his way in life by the speed of his gun hand and the coldness of his remorseless heart. Life never meant much to him until the world fell apart and they awoke. Overnight, the dead stopped being dead. Hungry corpses rose from blood splattered streets and graves. Their numbers were unimaginable and their need for the flesh of the living insatiable.

The United States is no more. Washed away in a tide of gnashing teeth and rotting, clawing hands. Dilouie no longer kills for money and pleasure but to simply keep breathing and to see the sunrise of the next dawn. . . And he is beginning to wonder if even men like him can survive in a world that now belongs to the dead?

www.severedpress.com

TIMOTHY
MARK TOFO

Timothy was not a good man in life and being
undead did little to improve his disposition.
Find out what a man trapped in his own mind
will do to survive when he wakes up to find
himself a zombie controlled by a self-aware
virus.

www.severedpress.com

35076817R00092

Made in the USA
Middletown, DE
18 September 2016